TWISTED

N GRAY

VINCI
BOOKS

By N Gray

Shifter Days, Vampire Nights & Demons in Between

Twisted

Lady Hawk and Her Mountain Man

Hidden Shifter

Wolf

Wolf Retreat

Night Hunter

The Fixer

Kai

Lee

Flynn

Jude

Scout Thorne

The Secret Tomb

Murder of Crows

Blaire Thorne

Ulysses Exposed

Voodoo Priest

Butterflies and Hurricanes

Salvation

Underworld Legacy

www.ngraybooks.com

Vinci Books

vinci-books.com

Published by Vinci Books Ltd in 2026

1

A CIP catalogue record for this book is available from the British Library.
Paperback ISBN: 9781036702175
The EU GPSR authorised representative is Logos Europe, 9 rue Nicolas Poussion, 17000 La Rochelle, France contact@logoseurope.eu

Chapter One

JULIA

All I wanted was an envelope. One stupid envelope to send a birthday card to my cousin. Instead of finding an envelope, I found this... documents about things I should never know about. This could get me killed.

Ice filled my veins, sweat beaded my forehead as I slowly closed the drawer. At first I expected the typical screeching sound when metal scraped against metal and was thankful I barely heard it close and relieved nobody else would either.

"What are you doing in my office?" Desmond's voice boomed behind me. His tone filled with rage.

I froze, swallowed hard, and slowly turned around. I fisted my hands as I glanced up at his hard face, finding nothing loving or caring about his expression. It was all hard lines and cold features.

My mind raced with things to say, to spew excuses for being in his office, but there was nothing. He had caught me with my hands in his things.

"Ah..." I muttered, swallowing the rest of my sentence as he approached with purpose.

"I've told you never to come in here." He scowled as he gripped my upper arms, yanking me away from his desk. He squeezed tightly, sending bursts of pain up my shoulders; hard enough to leave bruises.

"I was looking for an envelope—"

"Why?"

"It's my cousin's birthday, and I wanted to send her something."

"You shouldn't have opened my drawers, Julia. Do you understand the magnitude of your disobedience?" he said through gritted teeth, and the muscles in his jaw ticked. I'd never seen him this angry before.

"Yes…" I whimpered, averting my eyes. "Please don't hurt me, Des. I saw nothing." I lied. Obviously, I'd never tell him I saw the documents with multiple replicas they sold in Bill's art gallery. And I definitely wouldn't tell him I saw the name of the artist they commissioned who forged the paintings.

"I'm disappointed, Jules. I really am." He shoved two fingers painfully into my chest, pushing me into his filing cabinet.

I moaned on impact.

He raised his hand, but before he could strike, his cellphone sounded. "Huh, saved by the phone. Get out but don't go far."

"Yes, Desmond," I said meekly, hurried past him and closed his office door behind me.

I didn't want to stay outside his door and upset him further. Instead, I ran to our bedroom and closed the door quietly. I leaned against the door, pressing my palms against the cool surface, relieved I no longer stood in front of him and the object of his anger.

The other bruises had faded, replaced with new ones.

My emotions ran high, and I flinched every time he raised his voice.

His rage had worsened the last couple of weeks. Something at work was stressing him out, and he took it out on me. But this… this was my fault. I shouldn't have gone into his office. He warned me. I should've known better.

My breath hitched. My head throbbed as I pressed it into the hard door. The pain felt right. I deserved it, as I sucked in another breath—holding it. The moment I exhaled, I cried.

I needed to think.

Desmond had warned me never to enter his office without him being present, and that's exactly what I did. He wasn't home, and I thought I could quickly look for an envelope, but he'd come home before I found one.

The longer I thought about it, the more I realized there had to have been a silent alarm I'd triggered when I entered his unlocked office. He'd just left when he rushed back home. If he wanted me not to go inside, he should've locked it. But I'd never say that out loud.

I flinched when he knocked on the door. "Julia?" His tone wasn't as sharp as it was earlier. Perhaps he'd calmed down.

"Yes?" I whispered, squeezing my eyes shut.

The door handle turned as he opened the door, but I was leaning against it, keeping it closed. My eyes shot open as I turned around. The consequences of not opening the door would only make my situation worse. Slowly, I stepped away from the door. I barely had time to move out of the way when he pushed the door open, smashing it in my face. The impact threw me off balance and I fell backward, landing on my backside with a loud groan.

Pain shot up my spine from landing on my coccyx, and

my face ached while my eyes teared. My hand came away with blood; my nose didn't feel broken but it would be bruised.

Desmond stood in the doorjamb, his large body imposing and bathed in sinister shadows. He stepped forward, towering over me.

"You really shouldn't have gone into my office, Jules." His tone was deep and frightening. All the hairs on my arms stood on end.

"I'm sorry." I raised my left hand near my face on instinct; unsure if he'd hit me again or if he had thought I'd suffered enough. I never could tell.

"It's okay," he whispered. His change in tone kept me on high alert; it could mean anything. "It's going to be okay. I spoke with Bill and I made it right again. He won't punish you. And nothing bad will happen while I'm around. See, everything I do, I do it for you. Don't you love me when I do so much for you? When I care so deeply?"

I nodded, then flinched when he reached for my head, but instead of pulling my hair, he caressed my head. His touch filled with warmth and kindness, and I leaned into his hand. This was the Desmond I loved; the kind and gentle man.

"I saw nothing, Des. I promise. I really only wanted an envelope."

"I know, and it's okay. I found one for you, here." He handed me a white envelope. I took it with a shaky hand. "Next time, come to me first. You know I will go out of my way to get anything for you. Okay?" He reached for my hands and pulled me to my feet. "There you go. Put some ice on your nose to stop the bleeding," he said. His words were kind, but the undercurrent of his tone was not.

"How far are you with the books I gave you?" he asked,

placing both hands on my shoulders and applied just enough pressure. He pressed on the fading bruises that still hurt, but I dared not cower—he hated when I moved away from him.

"I'll get it done in two hours."

"Good." He squeezed my shoulders once more, then kissed my cheek. His stubble scratching my skin. "Thank you for doing it at short notice." His smile ticked to one side. I could tell he was toning down his irritation. "Bill is also grateful for what you do for the business. You have an hour to finish them."

"Okay," I whimpered. I made the mistake of asking for an extension, I learned my lesson and wouldn't ask for another one. I'd ensure I finished on time. "Must I make dinner?" I asked, averting my eyes.

"No, you can fix yourself a sandwich if you're hungry. No," — he shook his head, — "you'll eat a salad. Bread is bad for your waistline. I have a business dinner I need to attend now, so I'll be home late." He let go of my shoulders. I dared not look up while under the weight of his gaze. "And Julia, it's going to be all right." He pulled me into the curve of his body and kissed the top of my head. "Des always fixes your nasty messes."

Chapter Two

JULIA

I showered and scrubbed my body until I was red and rinsed thoroughly. The old bruises on my shoulders had darkened from Desmond squeezing so hard, but at least I could cover it with a three-quarter sleeve top. I applied makeup to the already fading bruise on my cheek and my friend Bailey wouldn't know the difference.

I double checked the work Desmond had left me, and it was complete and correct. I doubted he would find fault. I was thorough with my work and my books always balanced. But it never hurt to check.

I left a note on the kitchen counter in case he came home before me. But since he was attending a late dinner meeting, I didn't think he'd come home before ten.

My friend Bailey had asked for an early dinner since we hadn't seen each other in over a month. She said she had good news for me. I needed to hear something good—especially today. I wanted to forget about my life. Listening to her was just what I needed.

I arrived at *Magic & Beans*, one of the best coffee shops

in Sterling Meadow, found a parking spot near the entrance, and climbed out of my car.

Bailey sat at one of the outside tables and waved as I approached.

"Hey, hun. How are you holding up?" she asked, bringing me in for a hug. Her hugs were always exactly what I needed; filled with warmth, safety, and comfort. The smell of spring flowers and camomile tea wafted near her. She stiffened in our embrace and I wasn't sure what I did wrong.

"I'm fine—"

"No, you're not," she said, pulling away. "Something happened again, didn't it?" She held my shoulders and squeezed. I winced and tried to step away, but she held on. Her hands warmed. Her heat touched my skin through my clothing and burned down my arms.

"Ow," I moaned as my shoulders ached, followed by pins and needles shooting down to my fingers.

"He grabbed you again, didn't he?" She let go and sat down. A scowl crossed her usual pleasant features, and I knew she was mad.

I sat across from her, still rubbing my arms. My skin tingled as my neck and cheeks heated.

"I hate how you can sense things."

"I'm an excellent witch," she said with a smile and kind eyes.

"Nice hair. When did you have it done?" Last week her hair was lime green, today it's electric blue, reminding me of a mermaid I'd once seen when I was a kid.

"You like?" she asked, twirling a strand around her finger.

"Beautiful," I beamed at my friend. I was grateful to

have her in my life. No matter my mood, she always made me feel better.

I told her about my work, avoiding the '*Desmond subject*'. I knew how she felt. We had this discussion many times before. I didn't want to have it again.

Bailey told me about adding a few more clients to her 'consulting' business; a business where she helped others exact revenge on those who were deserving; mostly adulterers and bullies.

Bailey had potent spells she'd give to her clients to use on their '*target*' which taught them a lesson. Nobody died, and it was never permanent. But it made her clients feel in control of their lives and boosted their self-confidence and morale.

I laughed uncontrollably when she told me one client mispronounced the name and her '*target*' ended up with a wolf's tail for a month.

She also had clients who came to her for readings, and Bailey only used her gifts for good and empowerment; never for evil doing.

After we ate and enjoyed dessert, Bailey picked up her coffee and stared at me over the rim of her mug. I knew what she was dying to ask, but I always avoided the subject. We did not discuss Desmond... ever.

My relationship with Desmond was never this volatile before. I couldn't help but think it was partly my fault; I pushed him when I shouldn't and he was always nice to me afterwards. Bailey hated that. She said he was manipulative and abusive.

"I can't do this anymore, Jules. The man is going to kill you one day," she whispered, so only I heard. The nearby patrons too preoccupied with their own conversations. I doubted anyone cared about ours. "I know he sometimes has you followed," she continued, but her lips barely moved from behind her mug—reminding me of ventriloquists. "I've been thinking about this for a while and may have found a way of protecting you." Her eyes danced across the other patrons enjoying their late lunches. Then she turned her deep brown eyes on me, boring into my soul. "If Desmond threatens you, or you seriously fear for your life. I've already prepared the spell for you." She handed me a crumpled piece of paper, alerting no one to the fact. "Just say the words."

I chewed on my thumbnail as I read the words. "I'm not a witch. How will the incantation work for me?" I asked, although I wasn't sure I wanted to say the words anyway. Being with Desmond was comforting. Sure, he had his bad days, we all did. I didn't think I could have someone hurt him.

"The Demon Lord owes me a huge favor and he'll come to you the moment you summon him by saying the words. He will protect you with his life, Julia. When I say he owes me, *he owes me*." She arched both eyebrows. "He'll do what's necessary to get you out of there safely. If it's what you want. You do want it, don't you?"

I shrugged. My chest tightened at the thought. Desmond wouldn't let me go, he wouldn't allow me to just leave, especially since I did so much for his company.

Bailey sensed my conflicting emotions.

"It's the only way you can get away from that asshole," she grumbled. "You know he isn't good for you, and I know you're scared. He will stop you from leaving him. Abusers are like that. They manipulate you into thinking you need them. But you don't. You have me and you can stay with me again." She exhaled, red blotches marked her face as her anger slowly seeped away. "Next time he'll kill you." Her eyes flitted to my shoulders; the bruises hidden by my clothing.

I knew her words were true, but I still needed to believe them. It was hard for me to comprehend I could continue without Desmond. That I could get back on my feet. And being alone wasn't the same as lonely, but a choice to remove myself from harm. I knew all this... but... I struggled... perhaps with Bailey's help, I could.

"If I say these words, will the Demon Lord kill him?"

She shrugged. "He can, and he might. If Desmond tries to stop you from leaving, he will." She finished her coffee and set her mug on the table. She crossed her arms and gave me a deadpan expression.

She had thought this through. It was clear she hated Desmond. I loved him. But he scared me. He had hurt me a few times, but nothing so serious I needed a trip to the emergency room. Yet.

Desmond had anger issues that would trip him up quickly, but he always said 'sorry' afterwards and begged for forgiveness. He was always sincere in his apology. I knew he loved me.

I glanced at the crumpled paper again, unsure how a Demon Lord could help, but I'd hold on to it. I tucked it into my jean pocket and sipped my coffee.

———————

When the clock struck eleven, Desmond still hadn't come home.

I'd just fallen asleep when the front door opened and slammed shut. I waited for him to enter our bedroom and to assess his mood, but after two minutes had passed, he didn't show.

There were strange murmurs somewhere near the front of the house. Then muffled voices set my alarm bells off. I couldn't tell if they were arguing or just speaking in hushed tones.

I pulled on my robe and opened the bedroom door.

"Desmond?" I called above a whisper.

"Oh, hey," Desmond said as he entered the hallway so I could see him, then he added, "Bill's here." He thumbed behind him.

A dark shadow moved behind Des. I froze to the spot and reached for my upper left arm, feeling the scar. A deep scar Bill had inflicted with his sharp claws when I tried to walk away from him while he was speaking. He didn't appreciate anyone walking away from him. He taught me a lesson by inflicting pain and leaving me a memento; every time I saw him, I'd remember what he did.

I sucked in a deep breath.

"Hey, Bill. How are you?" I said as I calmly traversed down the hallway towards them.

"Julia!" Bill's tone was ominous and struck a chord within me, leaving me speechless. He licked his bloody lips. My eyes flitted from Bill's mouth to Desmond's neck; the wound already healed by vampire saliva.

Desmond was a blood-servant for Bill only. In exchange for being a regular blood donor, Desmond received other benefits; improved health, longevity, a salary and security; all this for a few sips of blood a few times a week.

Desmond rubbed his crotch. His eyes darkened as his pupils dilated—no doubt Bill's bite was sensual. I was sure there was something else going on in their *work* relationship, but I never asked. I doubted they'd tell me anything, anyway.

Bill wanted me to be his blood-slave, too, and I refused

him without thinking about it. I didn't want to be passed between masters in exchange for their addictive blood. I'd never tasted vampire blood before, nor would I ever—if I could help it.

"Desmond says you might have read something belonging to me?"

"I was only looking for an envelope."

"And did you find one?" Bill asked, arching a black eyebrow. Bill was a head taller than me, with black hair and eyebrows, and gray/silver eyes. His skin was pale and his features sharp. He hardly showed any emotions, which kept everybody on edge. Even Desmond.

My eyes flitted to Desmond, then back to Bill as his dark gaze raked up and down my body. I hated how he did that —making me uncomfortable by his stare alone—and so quickly.

"Ah, no, but Desmond came home and found one for me," I said, wiping my palms on my gown. My smile wavered at the sides and I knew Bill sensed my fear. I suspected my fear had a sour smell to it; I stood before Bill many times and knew I smelled like that every time.

"What did you see, Julia?" Bill's tone was crisp and unforgiving as he stepped closer. Dark shadows played on his features, his eyes seemingly more metallic than gray.

Instinctively, I stepped backward. But Bill was too fast for me. I barely saw him move. He gripped me by the throat and shoved me against the wall. I clutched at his wrist, trying to pull his hand from my neck. He squeezed until my pulse thundered in my ears. I couldn't breathe. My eyes bulged. Stars clouded my vision. Bill's features morphed as the darkness swept over him, leaving his true, twisted, demonic self.

I glanced at Desmond, who stood behind Bill with his

arms folded over his enormous chest, wearing a smile, his dark eyes glistening; he was just as twisted as his boss.

"Please," I breathed. My vision tunneled. Darkness swarmed around me. My chest ached. And my head felt as though it was about to pop off.

Bill finally let go and I crumpled to the floor. My limbs were numb and unable to keep me up as I landed with my butt on the floor and slumped against the wall. I sucked in a deep breath. Slowly, my limbs came alive and I rubbed my aching neck.

"It's only because Desmond loves you I haven't killed you already, *human*. I don't like it when someone snoops in my drawers."

I already knew it was Bill's drawers because of the documents with the painter's name and the paintings he'd forged.

"Ah, there we have it. You've realized, haven't you? So you did read inside—"

"I didn't I swear. I saw nothing. And if I did, I wouldn't say anything to anyone." I hated how my face sometimes gave me away.

They took part in organized crime, and it was lucrative. I suspected if anybody tried to intercept, Bill would have them dealt with swiftly. But what bothered me the most, with modern dating and analysis techniques, surely it would make the identification of forged artwork that much simpler. The people buying these paintings most likely trusted Bill blindly, or there's another reason, possibly money laundering.

"I know." Bill crouched in front of me; his aftershave assaulting my senses along with that copper stench. He reached for my face and I dared not move or he'd rip my throat out so quickly I wouldn't know what hit me, then he'd lap up my blood. "So pretty, and so clever, especially that memory of yours." He tapped the side of my head.

I pulled away then. I hated when someone tapped me on my head. It reminded me of school when the bullies hit me, taunted me, and sang, *'Dumb-dumb, Julia is a dumb-dumb.'* I was not stupid. School bored me. I knew every word in every textbook and could recite it word for word. All they had to do was give me the page number, and I'd tell them. But I was also lazy and never did my homework.

"Don't do that—"

"She hates it," Desmond said, tapping Bill on his shoulder. "She won't say anything. Will you Jules?"

I shook my head but kept my eyes on Bill. His eyes glowed red, and I was sure I wet myself; I couldn't be sure since my body felt numb.

"Go to bed. And if I hear you've done something like this again, I'm coming for you." Bill promised, and stood up in one swift motion. But he didn't move away. He towered over me like the dangerous vampire he was, ensuring I never forgot his threat.

I did as instructed and ran to our bedroom, slamming the door shut. I jumped into bed, covered my body with the duvet, and cried until I fell asleep.

My dreams came soon thereafter, and they were always the same...

I sat at my favorite coffee bar, Alpha Coffees, enjoying a cappuccino and a bran muffin when Desmond entered the shop. His charming smile held promise of something more, something dangerous yet alluring.

He couldn't tear himself away as his eyes raked up my body, leaving me hot and bothered.

Nobody had ever looked at me that way. He set all the alarms within me ringing and I didn't want him to stop. I didn't heed the warning.

Once he had placed his order, he asked if he could sit at my table. I graciously agreed; we had greeted each other before but this was the first time he joined me at my table. We spoke about anything and everything.

Desmond was an influential businessman, and I had just started working at an accounting firm. He grinned when he told me he needed an accountant and asked if I wanted to earn double my current salary. I almost choked on my coffee.

If I earned double my salary, I could pay off my student loans quicker and save for a house of my own. Living with my witchy roommate was wonderful, and we had fun, but it was still her apartment. I wanted a place of my own.

Desmond promised me the moon and so much more.

I was full of smiles with plans of my own and agreed to join Desmond's company.

The first week was wonderful. His books were easy to balance, and I saved him money on his taxes.

To celebrate, Desmond took me out to a French restaurant and ordered the most expensive food and drink. We ate, drank champagne, and spoke all night long. He was so romantic and kind. Before I knew it, I was in his bed, screaming his name.

Two days later, I moved in with him.

But by then it was too late.

Being the honest and trusting person my parents had taught me to be...

I didn't see the warning signs.

Chapter Three

JULIA

The next morning, I awoke to a quiet house. Desmond hadn't come to bed and had most likely gone to Bill's underground nightclub. He slept there often.

I ensured the house was clean. I double checked our room was spotless and smelled like flowers. The way Desmond preferred.

I ate quietly in the kitchen; a ham sandwich with a glass of milk. I should've eaten a salad, but Desmond wasn't home. He wouldn't know. While I ate, I thought of Bill's threat and knew Bailey was right. I couldn't stay here.

Bailey had offered me my old room back since it was still available. I could stay with her until I got back on my feet, even if it took me a year. At least I had a place. Some women didn't. Some had nothing and still got away from their abuser and made things work.

I needed help getting away; not only from Desmond, but from Bill, too. Both would come after me. I knew too much and had seen things I shouldn't have. I needed someone powerful enough against them. A Demon Lord seemed like the right supernatural to do that, and from what Bailey had said, this one was capable.

I had twenty minutes before I started the process. Just thinking about saying the words made me nervous. I wasn't a witch and never indulged in the arts, but I trusted Bailey. She had been by my side since forever and was doing everything in her power to help me. I owed her so much. But the thought of summoning any demon—Lord or not—left a foul taste in my mouth.

During my school years, they taught us never to interact with demons. Ever. They were evil and did everything in their power to get what they wanted. They were conniving, narcissistic, and power-hungry. I didn't know how Bailey befriended a Demon Lord or what she did for him to owe her a favor—but I trusted my friend. And I knew in my heart I had to go through with it if I wanted to survive Desmond and Bill.

Desmond knew of my eidetic memory. As much as I wanted to forget them, I would always remember the documents I read yesterday even after five, twenty years from now. I would remember every word.

I didn't have proof, but I knew what they were doing. If the authorities found out they had a witness—me—Bill would destroy me so quickly, I wouldn't see him coming.

I needed to remember he was as twisted as they came. And with that in mind, and to protect myself, I needed to gather some evidence to use against them as leverage.

After I finished lunch and cleaned the kitchen. I walked through the house one last time. I tried the front door, but

Desmond had locked it from the outside. He had never locked me inside his home before.

He also boarded up the windows; only slivers of sunlight squeezed through the cracks. I wondered what the house looked like from the outside. Desmond had never closed the shutters before either.

Everything about this day left me on edge. The thought of not seeing tomorrow was my reality today. The possibility of Desmond and Bill preparing to remove me from this earth became real.

If I was going to do this spell, I had to say it now while I still had a chance.

I grabbed the knife from the kitchen, along with the items I needed for the incantation. I set everything in the living room and pulled out the crumpled piece of paper.

Bailey had said all I had to do was read the incantation. I'd called her earlier to read it back to her since the pronunciation of the words left me tongue tied. She corrected me and instructed not to mess them up again. I had to say the lines in that order and pronounce each word properly.

"What would happen if I mess it up?" I had asked.

"You won't mess it up. Sit inside the circle of salt for protection, cut your hand, and read the words. It's easy." She had sounded way too calm.

The thought of messing up left my heart stuttering in my chest. My clothing clung to my body and sweat peppered my forehead.

I was not comfortable reading these foreign words. My memory was excellent, but saying words in another language was different and the chances of me messing up were great.

"Can't you come help me?" I had asked Bailey, even

though I doubted she could get inside. Desmond had taken my house keys.

"No, you must bind him to you. If I helped, I might bind him to me and I don't want that."

"Why? What's wrong with him?"

"Nothing is wrong with him…" she was quiet for way too long, most likely counting to a hundred. "You need the protection, that's all. Listen, I have to go. A client is waiting for me. Call me when you're done." She had ended the call before I protested.

Right! This was going to go wrong quickly, I just knew it.

I inhaled deeply, closed my eyes, and shook my shoulders. I could do this—I had to do this. If I waited any longer, I might not be around anymore.

I picked up the salt and drew a circle big enough for me to dance in. Then, once I was sitting inside, I reached for the knife. This was a blood spell binding the Demon Lord to me. But Bailey designed this spell in such a way that she could remove the bond once I was safe.

With the knife in one hand and the crumpled piece of paper in the other, I was ready. Sweat dripped down my back. My breathing came in short and shallow. I stared from the knife to the paper and my mouth was dry and my body numb.

"Oh gosh, well, here goes," I mumbled to myself. "What did Bailey say again? Should I cut myself first and then say it, or do I start the words and then cut?" I couldn't remember what she'd said.

The clock ticking behind me grew louder. Glancing over my shoulder, it was twelve on a Saturday afternoon, which meant Desmond always came home around this time. I had to hurry.

I closed my eyes and exhaled. I had to do this. I could

do this. And the moment I relaxed and gave in to the notion, everything fell into place. The order I had to do it and the words I needed to say. Everything.

I cut my left palm and watched my blood drip to the ground near my crossed legs. I glanced at the paper in my hand and read the incantation.

After I said the first sentence, I felt a jolt of power in the room. Dark shadows animated the house. The sun reflecting off a surface splashed through the cracks in the window. Followed by the sound of a car driving up our driveway.

Shit, Desmond was here.

I read the next line. The power thrummed. My pulse thundered in my ears. I read the following line, but I'd already read that line. Furrowing my brows, I realized I'd missed the second line and read it quickly. Then I read the third line and quickly said the fourth and last line.

The sound of keys jangling outside as Desmond neared the front door.

Glancing back at the paper, I skimmed over the lines and read the last word. I stuttered as I said the demon's name, hoping I pronounced it right.

The power pulsed in the room, blowing my hair back. I felt the pull of dangerous magic. My body hummed. The room shook.

I collapsed onto the floor. Fire seared through my veins. My thoughts crashed wildly. I couldn't understand why the Demon Lord wasn't here to protect me.

The front door opened.

I screamed.

But Desmond didn't see me and walked right past me. His face filled with confusion as he saw the items on the ground.

Twisted

I glanced at my hands as I dissolved into nothing.
It was then I realized I did something wrong.

Chapter Four

os

I leaned against the wall and watched her sleep. Her steady breathing relaxed me and the tension between my shoulders eased.

If I didn't know any better, I'd think I was in a Japanese apartment instead of a woman's bedroom in warm South Africa. Jennifer's room was spacious and sparse. In the corner stood a bonsai tree. There were no photos on the walls or on her oak bedside table, and the walls painted a calm yellow.

I crept towards her platform bed and dragged down the covers. My sleeping beauty wore white panties and a vest. She shivered, the cool air caressed her naked flesh.

Jennifer was breathtakingly beautiful lying on her side. Her dark hair a stark contrast against the white pillow. Her fair features held youth but sorrow. I felt sorry for her. A woman like her should be with someone, yet she's alone for me to take.

I nestled myself behind her. The heat from her body against my front made me shiver. I kissed her neck gently, eliciting a reaction from her; prompting her to push her ass against my front. I loved this part; making her do things that fed my hunger.

I walked my fingers down the side of her body, over her hips and down her leg, leaving goosebumps in my wake.

Jennifer stirred, moving her left leg farther over her right until her knee was on the mattress; her legs apart. The perfect pose with a magnificent view.

I walked my fingers back up her leg, heading for that sweet spot, where I brushed my fingers lightly against her delicate folds over her damp panties. She moaned, delighting me.

"Hmm, that's right, give me your essence, my love," I purred against the shell of her ear.

Her body stiffened. Her eyelids shot open, and she groaned. She felt me behind her; that there was someone else here with her, but she couldn't fathom who or what. But she knew something was wrong, unable to move, and couldn't understand why.

It helped if they couldn't see me. They'd feel my presence. Nothing more.

All they heard was their hard breathing and racing heart. They sensed something different—something not human—and blame it on the dream they had as a way to process their confused and sensual thoughts.

And they always craved release; their arousal sometimes caught them off guard, especially since nobody was around them when it happened. And that's where I came in, to nudge them in the right direction.

I sucked air over my teeth, scenting her. Awaking my inner demon. A change in the atmosphere as I felt her arousal stir deep within me. I caressed her delicate area once more; she shivered and closed her eyes; the delicious sensations of my power crashing into her.

I needed another shot of her essence to sate my hunger.

"Hmm, that's it, my dear. Give in to me. Take what you crave and give me what I need," I purred against her cheek.

Jennifer whimpered as she shuddered. The little orgasm I gave her without effort would keep me full for the day. Until tomorrow… and then I'd be with the next woman; never feeding on the same one twice. I wasn't cruel, and never killed. I only pleasured.

Jennifer groaned and her eyes rolled into the back of her head. She was very easy to please. Her lover would be very lucky to have her.

Then, as soon as the moment ended, I sensed something else, someone else around us.

The darkness pulling me back.

"No, I'm not done," I groaned, gripping the bedsheets.

Before I tasted more of Jennifer, the power of the Underworld sucked me back home.

Chapter Five

os

"What the hell?" I groaned as I landed face first on my bedroom floor.

Someone had yanked me away from my feast and slapped me back in the Underworld. Only powerful demons could do that, and I had angered none. Whoever did this was unknown to me, or the reason.

It was such a pity. I was having so much fun in South Africa. I had fallen in love with the city after my first visit. Seth had sent me to find and taste Ursula, the South African Child of the Sun everybody wanted their hands on. But, like always, the vampires swooped in and rescued her.

While I visited Cape Town the women had caught my eye. They were magnificent; all shapes, sizes, and color. All waiting for me to devour them. I licked my lips, thinking about the ones I'd already tasted.

"Oh, hi," someone said behind me; a very female someone. With a voice so sweet I could eat her for breakfast and not feel guilty.

I grunted as I slowly climbed to my feet, shaking my

head. I rubbed my sternum. My chest ached deep within, leaving me puzzled. The trip back had never caused this reaction before, making me wonder what went wrong. But I knew who had done it.

I turned around towards my visitor. My gaze raking up and down the female. My nostrils flared, her scent a delicate flower. Not only had this tiny woman with light brown hair and blue eyes summoned me to *my* room, but she did something *to* me. I rubbed my chest once more, but the burning sensation continued.

I blinked as my demon vision revealed moving ropes from her chest into mine. To the naked human eye, they'd see nothing, but to me it was a ghostly rope my hand could move freely through. It didn't hurt, but I felt it there—constantly—as it moved through her, through me, and back again. I felt her body and my own; like a foreign object connecting us—a parasite.

This couldn't be happening to me. I did nothing wrong and couldn't understand why I was being punished. A demon bound to a human was punishment for those deserving—I didn't deserve this.

Rage filled my veins, and my claws extended. "What did you do?"

"I don't know," she squealed, biting her nails. Her eyes glistening in the dim light with unshed tears. "I'm sorry, I don't even know how I got here—"

"What did you do?" I yelled and approached the tiny woman cowering in the corner. "You put a spell on me, binding yourself to me?" I towered over her shrinking form and she burst into tears.

"I'm sorry. I don't know what you mean."

Today was not going as planned. Either this was really a misunderstanding, or she's a talented actress. By binding me to her meant she could ask me to do things I normally wouldn't do. And I couldn't say no. She could make me her slave if she wished.

I needed to understand exactly what she had done so we could reverse it. And now.

"Where's the spell?" I reached for her hand. "Hand it over."

"The what?"

"Do you have a tiny piece of paper they wrote the incantation on?" I asked, my tone laced with sarcasm and malice.

The little mouse nodded, wiping away stray tears. She opened her hand, producing a crumpled piece of paper. I snatched it and opened it.

"Oh my gods, it's supposed to be Osmodos bound to you, not me." I said, trying not to laugh and cry at the same time. I couldn't believe it. It was just a simple mistake.

"Who are you, then if not Osmodos?"

"Os, but my real name is Osmodeus."

"Oh, no... no... no... your names are so similar."

"Yeah, but why my brother. What did he ever do to you?" I glowered down at the shaking little mouse and shook my head. "I can't believe you did this. How could you do it, anyway? I don't even sense anything witchy about you," I asked, waving the note.

"I'm not a witch, but my friend is. She helped me." Her tears continued streaming down her face, and she desperately needed a tissue. "She said the Demon Lord would help me. They had prearranged everything. All I had to was offer my blood and say the words."

Fuck!

I shook my head and crouched in front of her. For someone to bind a Demon Lord to them meant they were

27

in trouble. It was hard enough making a demon your friend; since most weren't agreeable. By knowing our names was a powerful tool the person could use against us, or have it sold to the highest sorcerer.

And knowing my brother, he would've agreed to do this willingly. He was just that kind of demon. *Asshole.* He always had to be the better son. I sighed audibly.

"Come on, princess, let me take you to O-s-m-o-d-o-s. Maybe he can sort this shit out."

Chapter Six

JULIA

After my world went dark, I landed in a room of someone's house. Shortly thereafter, a bright light flashed, and a creature appeared, lying face down on the floor. His skin looked hard, the color of deep purple. His tail swished behind him, reminding me of an irritated cat. He had to be the Demon Lord Bailey had told me about. But what I couldn't understand was why here. I should've been in Desmond's home, and the Demon Lord helping me escape.

My breath caught in my throat when he groaned and moved. I was sure he was going to eat me.

After he'd introduced himself and told me I'd made a mistake, I was so embarrassed. I couldn't believe what I'd done. I couldn't stop the tears as the weight of my incompetence crashed into me. Just another thing I'd failed in doing. Perhaps I was stupid after all.

"Come," he said, reaching for my hand with his clawed one. At first I hesitated, but eventually I slipped my hand in his. "I promise not to bite," he grinned, showing me his sharp pointy teeth.

I yanked my hand back, and he burst out laughing.

"Okay, I might bite. You're just so darn cute, like a little mouse. I want to nibble on your bottom lip, taste you." He snapped his teeth together. His dark gaze raked up my body and it was very sexual.

I squirmed, needing to get away from him. I stepped back until I hit the wall.

"Relax darling," he said, approaching the door. "I'm only teasing."

It was only as he walked away from me did I realize he was naked. His purple skin and tail had been holding my attention. When he turned around, I saw his front, my neck and face heated. He was not a shy demon and very aroused.

"Are you also a Demon Lord?" I croaked, cleared my throat, and stared at the floor.

"I am, but just a different flavor," he said seductively, making all the hairs on my body stand on end.

I swallowed hard. "Are there many types of demons?" I glanced up, meeting his black eyes. He had no pupils or irises, just black.

"Yep, we come in many shapes, sizes, and varying degrees of evil." He licked his lips with his forked tongue. I shuddered at the thought. Then he grinned, as if he knew what I was staring at.

"And are all demons purple?" I'd only heard about demons. I'd never spoken to one I could question.

"Honey, I can be whatever your heart desires." He stepped closer. I didn't like his closeness and tried to get away from him. But he was too quick. He pinned me in a corner; with a hand on either side of my shoulders. "Hmm, you smell good," he whispered, his voice silky smooth like velvet against my chest, and he moved closer. He brushed his nose against my right cheek, then the other, reminding me of a cat smelling their owners.

He leaned back, closed his eyes, and *changed*. His purple skin rippled like scales, leaving the color of pale ivory in its wake. His horns disappeared and now his head was full of sandy-brown hair cut short. Even his face changed, leaving him with sharp features and a chiseled jaw with stubble. When he opened his eyes, crystal blue eyes stared at me.

He stepped backward and twirled. His tight ass and sculptured muscles were everything I'd ever dreamed of.

Oh, gods, he read my mind.

"Yes, my dear, I am your wet dream in the flesh," he said, winking darkly. His smooth tone caressed my skin like butterfly kisses.

I swallowed hard and felt my mouth drop open again. "How can you do that? Is this what you always look like?"

"No, this is not my true form. But this is what you like," he said, a silent question.

I nodded.

He grinned. "Well, shall we see my brother?"

"Aren't you going to wear clothes?" I stared below his waist and heat pooled between my legs.

"Do I make you nervous?" He stepped closer. "Do you want to touch me?" He took another step towards me. "You're a shy one, aren't you? How about I touch you?" He closed the distance and stood so close his body pressed against mine; his heat beating against me. It would be easy to give in to my desires, to touch him.

I closed my eyes, wishing he'd go away. When he said nothing and I heard nothing. I opened my eyes. And stared at his naked chest. I groaned inwardly. He was tempting me. He was everything I desired in one neat and yummy package. But I couldn't and wouldn't give in.

"Don't worry, little mouse," Os said, stepping back. "Luckily, you brought us back to my place. I have something here I could slip on; if only to protect your innocence."

"I… I'm not innocent. It's just… you… that thing… you're walking around naked," I said, pointing at him and trying to maintain eye contact, but it was difficult.

He laughed, and headed into his walk-in closet, pulled a shirt and pants out and pulled them on sans underwear.

While he dressed, I had a good look at his bedroom; of all places I brought us here. To his private room where he did—*stuff*.

"I didn't know demons slept," I said, staring at his chest of drawers and then his unmade bed; silk sheets the color of blood. He had two mirrors on either side of his bed and a mirror on the ceiling. My mouth dried as visions of him and a woman flashed in my mind's eye. Salacious pictures of their carnal pleasures; her mouth on him, his fingers in her. My eyes shot open, and the sights disappeared.

"Oh little mouse, there's so much you still have to learn." He chuckled as he pulled his t-shirt down and slipped on sandals. "Come, the Demon Lord won't wait forever."

Chapter Seven

OS

I couldn't believe my luck. As much as I wanted to keep my guest locked up in my room, seduce her and fill every hole; it would've been such a treat. But, I couldn't bring myself to do it, I was a demon but I didn't take advantage even though others would. I wanted her to want me; she wasn't innocent, but that didn't mean she had experience. And I'd love to be the one to teach her every trick in my book.

And I loved how embarrassed she got every time she looked at me; at the body she'd conjured up in her mind. I glance down and grinned; I was a stud. I hadn't been this hunky in years, since I rarely changed my demon form to please a human these days. Usually I'd just stir women's arousal and feast on their delicious essence until I'd had enough. Messing around with women was better than getting to know them first. Ugh, I'd been down that road enough times to avoid. And every time I did. I vowed never again.

I only tasted them—I never killed... much these days.

Killing women was just a messy affair, and I hated

causing chaos with the humans. When that happened, shifters or vampires got involved, and everybody knew how bad their tempers were. And I wasn't in the mood to deal with any of them.

I was a lover when it came to matters of the heart—not a fighter.

It was always us demons against the rest of the supernaturals, and I'd much rather play and leave, then stay and kill while I fought my way out.

"Catch up, little mouse." I beckoned her with a crook of my finger. I chuckled, I'd love to make her come with this finger.

"Please stop calling me that. My name is Julia."

We traversed the Underworld hallways until we reached the portal. I stopped and waited for *Julia*, holding out my hand.

"Where does this go?"

"You want my brother, don't you?"

She nodded, glancing at the portal, then back at me.

"Then take my hand, darling."

She hesitated, staring at my larger hand.

"It's easier on your body if you hold my hand, otherwise you'll turn green and puke your lungs out. These portals are for demons, not weak humans." I arched an eyebrow and wiggled my fingers. She reluctantly held my hand, and we stepped through.

Unfortunately for little mouse, or rather Julia, she still puked... all over my feet. I slapped her back, helping her expel whatever else she ate, but I took great pleasure in smacking her. Payback for ruining my shoes.

"Feeling any better?" I grumbled, kicking off the sandals.

"Yes," she said, wiping her mouth with her sleeve. "Sorry about your shoes."

"It's fine, come. This way." I continued walking without waiting for her.

She ran to catch up, slipping her hand through mine again. I almost jerked away from her, but it was obvious she liked my big, powerful hand enveloping hers. I squeezed her hand and held firmly.

We entered through a doorway and into my brother's library. He was a complete nerd for a Demon Lord, but this was what he loved doing. He maintained order within the library and ensured the tomes were safe. If anybody removed a tome, he made sure they returned it swiftly—or 'off with their heads' as the Queen of Hearts said.

Osmodos kept the important tomes on shelves locked behind secret doors, he with the only key.

Osmodos was my older brother, and apparently wisest. It was only because he read words all day, every day. Sometimes he'd perform spells, using his magic. Yeah, he was powerful. But he preferred using his powers here.

"Ossie?" I yelled. "You have company."

"Os?" He replied, sticking his head around a dark wood shelf. His suspicious eyes shifted between me and Julia. "Who's the girl?"

"Today is your lucky day," I said, pointing at Julia. "You've won a prize."

His brows shot together in confusion. No doubt his mind was still in his books and had forgotten he had chores that needed tending today.

"Apparently you struck a deal with a human," I said, hopefully jogging his memory.

"Oh, shit."

"Yes, that '*oh, shit*'. Ossie, what were you thinking?" I grumbled.

Ossie replaced the tome on the shelf, wiped his claws on his scaled chest, and approached.

Ossie was a powerful demon, completely black with black/metallic scales. He stood almost double Julia's size in comparison. I watched her gawk up at him, unsure whether she should be afraid. And she should be.

Ossie had the ability to morph into a more appealing human form, but he rarely did that much since he stayed here most of his days monitoring history for the rest of us.

Julia squeezed my hand and moved behind me.

"Oh," Ossie said, realizing he frightened her. He slunk down to size and into his prettier human form; long, silky black hair tied in a ponytail, bright green eyes, and a charming smile. "It's okay, you can come out from behind my asshole brother."

Julia moved beside me, her hand still in mine, and very damp. I wanted to shake her off me but thought it best not to; she was already afraid. Poor mouse. Served her right for interrupting my nocturnal meal.

"I thought Bailey was going to give you the incantations?" Ossie asked.

"She did, but little missy messed it up. She summoned *me* and bound herself to *me*."

Ossie's eyes flitted from mine to Julia's. Then he roared with laughter. "Really? How did you get that right?"

I handed him the crumpled piece of paper to read.

"The words are correct—"

"My boyfriend was about to walk through the door and I panicked," Julia said. "I repeated the sentence I skipped and I think I mispronounced your name," she added, glancing up at me.

Both Ossie and I laughed until dark tears streamed down our faces. No matter what form we took, our tears and blood remained black—like our dark hearts.

"It's not funny." Julia stamped her foot, letting go of my hand, and folded her arms.

"I'm sorry, but in hindsight it's hilarious," Ossie said, grinning, then quickly schooled his features. "Don't worry, Julia, I'm sure we can sort this out. Can you tell me which sentence you said first or messed up? If I knew the order, I could see how to reverse it." He asked carefully, not wanting to upset her again.

She told him she'd said the first sentence correctly, then the third. When she had heard her boyfriend arrive, she quickly said the second one, the third sentence again and then the final one. And how she pronounced his name, which was actually my name.

"Bailey and I went over it so many times. But I still messed it up." Her voice quivered and her chin trembled and I felt sorry for the little mouse.

"It's going to be okay," Ossie said, throwing an arm around her shoulders and hugged her lovingly. She nestled under his arm, perfectly at ease now. He was so smooth, I almost praised him. "At least you're bound to Os," he grinned at me, wiggling his eyebrows. "He isn't all that bad. And apparently he wants to impress you with those hunky features," he chuckled.

I slapped his shoulder.

"I thought demons were cruel and deadly," she said, stepping away from Ossie.

We could've heard a pin drop it was so quiet. I heard Ossie's heart thump against his ribs, along with my own.

Poor Julia's heart was racing, trying desperately to get out of her ribs. Beads of sweat peppered her forehead as she glanced at Ossie, then at me.

I stared at my brother and assumed my expression looked just as shocked as his. I swallowed hard, and so did he.

"Uh, that's just the thing," Ossie said, nervously scratching his head. "Demons are usually somewhat vile, despicable creatures. The absolute worst. Killers, thieves, kidnappers, you name it. But, ah…" I suspected Ossie didn't know how much he wanted to share with our human friend. When his eyes flitted to mine, I offered a curt nod. "You see…" he started. "Our mother was a gentle soul—bless her. Os and I are more like her. And well, I was the one you should've summoned up there." He pointed at the ceiling, indicating Earth. "Then once I'd sorted out that jerk boyfriend, you'd release me with Bailey's help. What you've done with Os, is going to be tricky to undo. I'd have to do some research to reverse it. But here's the thing, no-one can know you're here. And neither of you can leave the Under-world until I figure out what to do."

"What?" Julia and I said at the same time.

Chapter Eight

JULIA

I think my head just exploded. My body trembled as a cold sweat covered my body. I needed to sit down and didn't bother with a chair. I crashed to the floor with a loud thud, not caring about my butt or that my hips ached. Perhaps I needed pain to know I wasn't dreaming. I wish I was dreaming, then I could wake up. But then my reality wouldn't be that different. Either way, it was a nightmare.

"Honey, we need to break the bond you've created with my brother," Osmodos, or rather Ossie, said. He crouched before me and held my hands.

Ossie, in his demon form, was nothing like his brother. Ossie was easily double the size of me, completely black, with black/metallic scales. The smell of sulphur wafted in the air; even when he was in human form. As a human, Ossie's eyes were a dazzling green in color, with silky long black hair tied in a low ponytail, and a pleasant face. He wasn't ugly or drop dead gorgeous. He reminded me of a junior lecturer with his tweed jacket and dark brown slacks —he even wore glasses.

I felt my frown deepen as I stared into his face. "Do you even need glasses to see?"

He smiled. "No, my eyes are perfect. I love the way I look with glasses on." He stood and twirled. "It helps my image here at the library."

His words made me chuckle; it was an odd thing to say. I wondered if anyone even came here. From their behavior, I could tell they were vain. But I'd never say it out loud. I didn't know what they'd do to me.

Ossie's expression softened and considered me with kind eyes. They were pretty eyes. They seemed to twinkle in the soft light of the library.

I glanced around, taking in the huge hall-type-room we were in. It was nothing like any library I'd seen back home. I didn't think any library anywhere looked anything like this one. There were rows and rows of bookshelves. They filled the walls with bookshelves and high ceilings. At certain places along the wall were thin walkways where you could easily reach the shelves, but there were also rolling ladders to move across the walkway for those higher to reach shelves.

Sconces burned with dim orange light against the walls. The chilled air brushed against my face, cooling me. With coal colored tiled floors beneath me, and against the far wall was a black spiral staircase reaching the roof and a door leading out, to somewhere I didn't know. The air smelled of fire and ink.

I stared into Ossie's human face and the panic I'd subjugated surfaced, followed by quick breaths. I didn't want to stay in the Underworld, I wanted to go back home.

"What do we do now?" I asked. The back of my throat ached as I tried not to cry.

"Well, we have to do something about your smell?"

Immediately, I lifted my arms, and both men roared with laughter.

"No, silly, not *that* smell. Your scent." Ossie kept my hands in his. "We need to keep you hidden. The others can't know you're here. If anyone sees you, you wouldn't last the day." Ossie's eyes flitted from mine, then to Os's.

"Don't lie to me. What will really happen if anyone knows I'm here?" I asked as a nervousness swept through me.

Os sat beside me and slowly rubbed my back. It was nice of him to soothe me, but I was trying hard not to freak out, but I needed to understand my predicament.

"Isn't she just sweet? I could eat her up." Ossie said and winked at me. "As delicious as you look, I won't take a bite, so don't stress," he grinned. He exhaled and sat cross-legged in front of me. "They filled the Underworld with various demons, most of which you don't want to meet. Ever. There are some, like Os and I, who have more love in our hearts than evil," he smiled, trying to put me at ease. "More importantly, we need to keep you away from Seth. He is the older brother of Victor, Lord of the Underworld. They are forever at odds with each other. Seth despises humans where Victor embraces them. If Seth found out we're harboring you, he'll end us no matter how much he likes us." He glanced at Os, their fear evident. "As for you, he will play with you first—not in a nice way—then end you."

"Shit, so this is a clusterfuck."

Both demons burst out laughing.

"You can say that again, little mouse," Os said. "Who are you going to ask about the binding?" He asked his brother.

"Bailey, she has to know how to sever these ties."

"How will you ask her?" I asked, glancing between the two demons.

"Luckily we have a direct line." He wiggled his eyebrows and stood up in one swift motion as if pulled on strings. "For now, Os, keep her safe. And Julia," he said, waiting for me to look up at him. "Os needs to mask your scent."

"How?"

"He will know."

I didn't like the sound of that, but it sure made Os's grin split his face in two.

Chapter Nine

JULIA

"No, I can't let you do it," I yelled, stomping away from Os.

"No demon will come near you, Julia. I promise. If my scent is all over you, it would literally repulse the other demons. If Seth finds out—"

"I know, I know," I grumbled, and flopped down on the leather couch. There was a fireplace with an angry flame licking the sides; like it wanted to get out. I wanted to get out.

"I'm not asking to sleep with you—"

"You might as well. It's gross," I shuddered.

"Do you want to die?"

"No."

"Good, then let me do this."

"You would love it, wouldn't you?"

"Of course I would. Who wouldn't love licking your skin and planting kisses everywhere," Os said, sitting beside me. "You have had sex before, haven't you?"

I glared daggers at him.

"And your partner has kissed you everywhere." He

43

pointed at my shoulder, my breasts, and somewhere near my hips. "And you've had a love bite somewhere?" He pointed at my neck, then back at my breasts. "I will even stay in this body. I know you like him."

I gave him a side glance and watched him slowly lift his shirt, revealing his tanned, honed body. Then he seductively touched his chest, enticing me, enthralling me. Not wanting to embarrass myself by asking a stupid question, but I thought Os might be an incubus. It was the only explanation I thought of that explained his actions; and that every time he touched me, a bolt of sensual energy passed between us. I didn't know the alternative if he wasn't an incubus, since I didn't know all there was to know about demons.

I tried to hide my smile while he flicked his nipples before pulling his shirt down again.

Os was everything I'd always wanted in a man. I'd dated a few guys before Desmond. They had mostly an athletic build with muscle. I liked men who looked after themselves and were physically and mentally strong.

Desmond was tall and bulky, with a slight paunch. Lately, he enjoyed his beers and oily foods, and hardly exercised. I'd told him enough times he'd die of a heart attack if he didn't start looking after himself again, but he always brushed it off like the vampire blood he drank would save him.

Os had transformed himself into the man I always imagined when I had sex with Desmond; the surfer-type-lifeguards with the bronzed skin, wavy sun-kissed blond hair and drowning-blue eyes. He was sex on a stick; exactly the reason I couldn't sleep with him. He was not real.

"And we're not having sex," I said, making sure he understood I meant it.

"I'd love to have sex with you. But no, all I'm going to do is kiss you, rub myself against you so that you don't smell like the human dessert that you are." His gaze held heat I'd gladly burn in. It felt wrong, yet strangely right at the same time. But I knew it was wrong, fake. My breath caught in my throat when a ripple of sensations struck my core, and I sat upright, scowling at him.

"Did you do that?"

"Honey, I can do a lot of things without touching you. But, it only works if you crave it. And clearly you do." He neared and undressed.

"Wait, you're going to do it naked?"

"Of course, and so must you. How else am I going to get that sweet stench off of your body?"

"I'm leaving my underwear on."

"You will only soil them." One side of his mouth curved upward.

"Argh," I moaned, feeling my cheeks heat.

"It's time to get naked." Os undressed slowly, ensuring I saw every muscle move beneath his skin. He flexed and moved with such dexterity my head would explode if I didn't stop ogling him.

I stood and turned my back on him and removed my clothing, folding it neatly and placing them on the coffee table. When I turned to face him, I stared straight into Os' broad chest. I had to look up since he was a head taller than me, but then something lower moved, catching my eye and I glanced down. His enormous erection stood at attention and inches away from me.

Oh gods...

"Did he do this?" Os asked tenderly, gently thumbing the bruises on my shoulders.

I didn't want to talk about them. Instead I just nodded.

"You're safe now," he whispered.

We stared at each other for a moment, neither moving, and it felt intimate. Unspoken words were shared; silent words that told me he cared and he'd help.

My shoulders relaxed and I exhaled.

"Lie down." He demanded. "You don't have to do anything you don't want to. You're welcome to go with the flow, move with my ocean if you like." He moved his torso like a wave, his pelvis moved closer towards me—along with his erection—and wiggled his eyebrows. "And if you want me to penetrate you, darling, tell me when. I'll gladly give it to you. Now, don't get spooked, but it will feel like I'm smothering you with my body, but we seriously need to get that sweet scent off of you." His tone was light and fun until the last part, that he said gravely.

I did as instructed and laid on the couch while Os climbed on top of me. First, he straddled my waist with that erection so close to my hands on my stomach. All I had to do was lift my hands, and I'd touch his steel member. The temptation was right there. But I bit down on my bottom lip and stayed still.

Then Os leaned over. I moved my hands to my sides while his erection pressed against my stomach—I felt it throb. He cupped my face and planted soft kisses on my cheeks, followed by a chaste kiss on my lips. He was gentle, his lips soft and caring. Every touch he filled with affection. He didn't know me, yet he did it with ease. I felt like the only one in his world. But I knew it was fake and this feeling would never last beyond this moment.

His fingers were slightly hard, yet he touched me with such endearment I wanted to cry. I hadn't enjoyed such company since I started dating Desmond. We only had one evening where Desmond showed his tender side. Once I was living with him, all I got was his darker, gloomy side. I starved for his affection, yet all I received in return was his hatred and meanness. Whether I was the cause or if Desmond was always like that, I'd never know. I didn't want to understand it anymore. I was through with him and needed to move forward.

Os pushed my head to the side and kissed down my neck, making all the hairs on my body stand up.

A strange rumbling sound came from him, reminding me of a cat purring. He continued his delicious assault on my body; planting kisses everywhere, eliciting soft mewling sounds from me.

"That already smells better," Ossie said, entering the library and drinking something steaming from a mug. "Hopefully, it will mask her for a while. Just stay by her side while I'm chatting with Bailey. That way they'll always smell your stink."

"I don't think I could leave her if I tried. I think the maximum distance I can move away from her is thirty feet, then I feel a powerful pull to get back to her. Not sure if she feels the same?" Os said, staring at me.

I shrugged. "I don't know. It feels like I'm having an out-of-body experience so I wouldn't know."

"We'll test it when we're done here," Os winked and continued nibbling a hip bone.

"Oh," I whimpered as he kissed near the apex of my legs. "Too low," I moaned, reaching for his head to get him away from that area. Heat pooled between my legs, and I wanted to squirm.

Os shifted, moving his hard body between my legs. "Open wider, darling. I need to get everywhere." He made himself comfortable between my legs without squashing me. He hovered above me on his elbows near my head, his face close to mine. "You have such pretty green eyes. There are flecks of yellow in there," he whispered seductively.

I couldn't respond as I felt his warm breath caress my face, leaving tingling sensations in his wake. His expression left me tempted as my body hummed with sensual power. I didn't understand my body's reaction to him, but it felt so good. My skin tingled. My core muscles clenched in ecstasy, and he had done nothing apart from butterfly kisses against my skin.

I needed to think of something else instead of Os's delicious assault on my body. I thought of numbers, books, and making them balance. Then I thought of Desmond, and that I no longer considered myself as his girlfriend. Desmond was cruel and only used me to do his books. I should've left him long ago. Now was the time to save myself; needing to get away from him and Bill before they hurt me. Unfortunately, I'd seen some things I shouldn't have and now I needed outside help to break free from the stronghold they had on me.

As I stared into Os' clear-blue eyes, I felt free. For the first time in a while, it felt as though my life was mine once more. I felt like I could breathe without needing to look over my shoulder, wondering whether I did something wrong.

In some strange, twisted way, perhaps binding myself to Os was a good thing. I hoped.

For now, I might enjoy what Os offered. *Why not?* I wasn't dead… yet.

On instinct, I reached for Os's face. He closed the gap and kissed me. His tongue pressed against my lips and I opened my mouth, allowing him entrance. He lowered his body and pressed his hard erection against my aching mound, grinding against my sex.

Our intense kiss left me breathless and wanting more. I

wanted his hot flesh against mine, filling me. He continued rubbing against me while his tongue assaulted my mouth. The conflicting sensations left a burning desire. I wanted more. I wanted all of him.

I lowered my hands to his broad back and felt his muscles move beneath his skin. I lowered my hands to the curve of his soft ass and squeezed. He smiled in the kiss and opened his eyes. I felt his stare, making me open my eyes. He pulled away, his smile morphed into a salacious grin, threatening to set my now wet panties on fire.

The sound of a door opening and closing echoed in the library. The heat from the fireplace beat against us.

Os stopped moving. "Shit," he said, moving to the front of me and pushing me behind him until he sandwiched me between him and the couchback. Os turned to face me, wearing a worried expression. "Whatever you do, don't say a word. Do you understand? Just nod."

I nodded, slowly coming back to myself as if dunked in freezing water. Now that Os no longer touched me, I could think clearly. Even though I no longer wanted to be with Desmond, that didn't mean I'd jump into the next guy's bed and so quickly. Whatever Os had done to me had started the moment he placed a hand on me. But now I shivered from the loss.

"Good." He kissed the top of my nose, grabbed the blanket to cover us, then turned around in time. "Seth! To what do we owe the pleasure?"

Chapter Ten

OS

I hated Seth.

He was as cruel as they came, the worst. But he was my master and ruled over most of the demons even though his brother, Victor, ruled the Underworld. And they had a long-standing feud since forever. Nobody knew what they were fighting about. But everybody wanted Seth's real name. I'd searched for his name for as long as I'd been around. When I eventually get it, I'd use it against him, destroying him.

"Os," Seth drawled, sniffing the air. "What in the devil's name is that smell?" There was a twinkle of recognition in his eyes and I almost flinched. If he noticed my hesitation, he'd know something was going on and demand my obedience. I needed to explain who Julia was without saying too much.

"This is my new slave," I offered, thumbing Julia behind me. "She's sleeping now—"

Seth roared with laughter. "That's odd don't you think? You haven't brought a slave here in some time."

It unnerved me that Seth sometimes knew what we did

down here. We didn't know the reach of his power, but we would never underestimate him.

"I enjoy having her around when I need her." I slapped her thigh and grinned.

Earlier, when I'd heard Seth's approach, I morphed back into my natural form. It made me seem more evil than the blond hunk Julia preferred. As much as I wanted to remain sexy for her, I had to change.

"I understand. Anyway, where's your brother? I need to ask him something."

I wrapped my tail around Julia's leg and kept my free hand on her thigh, squeezing her now and then for reassurance. I wasn't sure whether I'd scent marked her enough, but to me she smelled more like me than like the sweet meat she was.

"He stepped out for a short while, giving me some privacy."

Julia moved behind me and something flashed in Seth's eyes. He leaned forward. His dark eyes narrowing, trying to see behind me. His nostrils flared. I squeezed Julia's thigh again and leaned into her. I couldn't allow Seth to see her.

Seth stood straight, content, and fixed his coat. "Let your brother know I'm looking for him," he said with a hint of irritation. I didn't know what it meant, but it worried me.

"Sure, will do," I said, relaxing slightly.

Seth turned and headed for the exit; his large, heavy footsteps echoing in the library. Once I heard the door open and close did I exhale a shaky breath.

"Hun, we need to get out of here." I turned to face Julia again. Her eyes large, staring at me while she chewed on her thumbnail. "And stop that. You're going to lose it." I pulled her thumb out of her mouth.

I morphed back into the hunk she loved and stood up,

quickly dressing. I handed her clothing, and she, too, dressed.

Her body trembled as she pulled on her jeans and shirt.

"It's going to be okay," I said, squeezing her elbow. "There's a door over there," — I pointed towards the portal Os had used earlier to meet Bailey, — "it will take us where Seth can't find us."

"Okay," she nodded mechanically, clearly in shock.

"Hey," I touched her chin and lifted it, meeting her frightened eyes. "I won't let anything happen to you. Some may think I'm perverse, but I never hurt. Ever."

She nodded a few times as tears welled in her eyes.

Once she dressed, I reached for her hand and led her to the door. As I pulled down the handle, the door swung open with a demon standing in the doorway. His hardened molten skin smoked, his eyes silver and he wore a pointy smile that would make a human crap themselves. The demon stood before me, holding demonfire in his palm.

"Shit," I breathed, slamming the door shut and locking it. "Forget that way," I grumbled. "Come, let's go this way."

"Who was that?"

"One of Seth's lackeys. Don't worry, I know another way." I opened another door, coming head to chest with a monster of a demon. His scaly skin moved, sounding like metal grinding. He punched me in the chest, sending me across the library.

Julia screamed as the brute gripped her upper arm, burning her skin, pulling her towards him and through the doorway.

I bolted upright and sprinted after them. I lunged for the door before they disappeared. With everything I had, I reached for the brute's shoulders, missing him but gripped his coat then demonfire surrounded us.

Twisted

We landed with a hard thud inside Seth's chambers, with Julia still screaming.

Chapter Eleven

JULIA

I stopped crying when the huge demon let me go. A raging fire still surrounded him, and even his eyes were wild with flames. I was thankful to be alive and my clothing was intact, even though he was aflame when he'd grabbed me. When he stood on one side, I glanced at my surroundings and curious what we were waiting for. Then I saw Seth approach, and a nervousness swept through me like a hurricane.

Seth's dark coat billowed behind him. His wide shoulders almost reached either side of the corridor walls, and the doorframe tall enough to allow him through. He and Ossie seemed to be of similar height and I wondered whether most demons were that tall and shrank themselves down when humans were around so not to scare them. There was much I didn't know.

"I expected more from you, Osmodeus," Seth said as he entered the room. His tone laced with hate.

I glanced over my shoulder at Os, who was lying against

the far wall. He was back in his natural form; purple skinned, horns on his head, and soulless black eyes.

"You know I don't enjoy sharing." Os wiped black liquid from his mouth and slowly stood up. He approached, then stopped when Seth raised his hand.

"Stay there. I need to see this prize before you leave your stink on her." Seth approached me with purpose. His deep red skin shone. He had two large horns sticking out of his forehead, with pointy ears and sharp teeth. His eyes glowed yellow, reminding me of a snake.

I shuddered the closer he got and flinched when he bowed slightly, reaching for me. I recoiled when he grabbed a strand of my hair, bringing it close to his nose, then let go. He stood upright and his translucent third eyelid closed over his eye and opened again. He shrunk as he morphed down into a human sized man.

Seth's deep red skin blended into a honey undertone, with bright blue eyes and a pleasant face. His black hair grew out of his head and stopped at his shoulders. And his horns disappeared. He was now a head taller than me, but his colossal form still intimidating.

"What is a human doing here?" he asked, staring at me, but I knew the question was directed at Os.

I did nothing but stare at the imposing man, Demon King, or whatever he was.

I heard Os approach and stand behind me. "My Lord, she is my slave."

"I thought I told you to stay where you were." Seth raised his hand. I stepped back as a wave of his power smacked into me and threw Os against the far wall again.

A large hand grabbed my wrist, yanking me closer. I smacked into his broad chest with such force it relieved me that my reflexes still worked and my free hand hit him, stopping me from head butting his pec muscle. I quickly stepped back, trying to yank my hand free, but Seth held me in a vise-like grip.

He hissed as he pulled me closer again.

"You are not a slave," he seethed with anger. He glanced at Os again, while squeezing my wrist. "Try again, fledgling."

My arm tingled, followed by pins and needles. I tried to pull my hand back again, but Seth wasn't letting go.

Seth lifted his head slowly, reminding me of someone who was trying to listen to faint sounds. His eyes clouded to a silver color, then back to blue. He breathed over his now blunt teeth, as if tasting the air, and closed his eyes.

"She bound herself to you?" he asked, shaking his head. "Who would do such a thing?" He turned his dark gaze on me. I felt blood drain from my body. My wrist frozen in his grasp and my arm numb.

"Please let go of me," I whimpered.

Seth snapped his fingers, and a cage appeared behind me, followed by metal grinding. He pushed me towards the cage, raised his hand and flicked his wrist. The cage door sprang open, and he pushed me inside. Another flick of his wrist and the cage door closed.

"No, wait. You don't understand—"

"Don't I?" Seth yelled. His body enlarging as he changed back to his natural form; deep red skin, horns, and large black wings I hadn't noticed before. "Don't forget who you're addressing, fledgling. You forget, nothing happens under my roof without my knowledge." He approached Os, towering over him.

Dark shadows followed Seth, surrounding him, making him appear sinister. I thought I saw screaming faces in the shadows or if my eyes were playing tricks on me. Either way, it was haunting.

Seth grabbed Os by the neck, pushing him up the wall and choking him. He raised Os off the floor, so he could look him in the eye.

"She's mine!" Seth growled, squeezing Os's neck. I thought his head would pop off. But Seth let him go, and he crumpled to the floor. "You're lucky I've enjoyed my time with your mother and promised to keep you and Osmodos safe. Now go."

"She doesn't belong here, Seth. Allow me to find you another—"

"Get out!" Seth's voice boomed in my ears, threatening to deafen me. I covered my ears, but it was too late; they started ringing as my world slowed.

Osmodeus floated in the air, then he disappeared in a bright light, followed by backdraft of angry flames.

Chapter Twelve

OS

I wiped blood off my face, then punched my fist into the mirror. The shards sliced through my knuckles like a hot knife through butter and scattered in the basin and on the floor. This girl was a human, yet I felt the need to protect her, comfort her, own her. She was so soft and fragile; timid and meek. She needed someone like me to take care of her. And I just lost her.

I pulled another piece of glass out of my purple flesh, and more dark blood seeped out. Shaking my head, I couldn't believe I allowed Seth to get his claws on her. It wasn't as if I had a choice. He could easily destroy me.

It bothered me how he knew about her. But one thing was for certain: I had to get her back, break the bond and get her home—even if it was the last thing I did.

"Fuck!" I screamed, needing to hit something else.

"Is everything okay?"

I spun around to Ossie, leaning against the doorjamb with a smirk which slowly morphed into a scowl when he saw the blood.

"What happened?"

"Seth—"

"What?"

"Seth has her."

Ossie was quiet for a moment, deep in thought, then nodded once with a knowing smile.

"Don't worry," he continued. "While Bailey works on the spell, we'll break Julia out of Seth's chamber."

"How?"

"I have a few sigils I could use."

"I don't like that. What if Seth's there when you perform them?"

"The sigil won't work if he is. We need to free her undetected," he said as he paced.

It looked like he had more to say, but kept quiet. When he sensed me watching him, he stopped pacing.

"Now don't be mad, but I also went to Victor—"

"What? Now he wants Julia too, I suppose," I said, cringing.

"Surprisingly not. He has his hands, or mouth, already full of human *friends*. And besides, he hates Seth. He's the one who gave me the sigil which Bailey is amending. When she's done, we could use it to break Julia out of the Underworld."

Sigils and sorcery were not my thing. I could get myself in and out of the Underworld, fight, and make love, but me and incantations were not friends. I left that to Ossie. As much as I hated the idea of using a sigil Victor had given us, I trusted Ossie to see us through. And if he trusted Bailey, then so did I. But it left me worried.

"Don't worry so much, brother." Ossie squeezed my shoulder. "We'll get her back. I have a plan," he grinned.

"You're crazy," I said as we reached the other side of Seth's chamber. Footsteps echoed down the gloomy hallway. Ossie and I pressed ourselves against the walls, blending in. Seth moaned at one of his lesser demons as they traversed farther away from us. We waited until they disappeared before attempting this crazy plan.

"I know. Besides, we wouldn't be brothers if I wasn't," Ossie said, tracing blood sigils on the wall.

"He's going to kill us."

"Hopefully not. We're his best. Without us, and apart from his children, he has nobody powerful enough to do his work," Ossie said as the blood sigil glowed red.

We stared at the glowing sigils and braced ourselves. We'd use it to open a doorway into Seth's chamber and the cage he'd locked Julia in. The plan was to help her escape, then get out of the Underworld.

Demons punished by Seth never came back. He ensured he ripped their souls from their bodies in the most violent way, then he tortured them every minute of the day for eternity. I wasn't looking forward to that.

Chapter Thirteen

JULIA

Seth morphed back into his dark human form and removed his leather coat. He rounded his shoulders and rolled up his sleeves while staring at me. It was unnerving. I cowered in the cage's corner, bum on the floor, wrapping my arms around my knees.

The fear I had for Desmond and Bill was nothing compared to the fear I had for Seth. This demon was something else. He made every part of me want to scream and run away, or die trying.

I averted my eyes for fear he would approach and glanced around his chambers. The first thing that caught my eye was his neatly made bed. It had black silk bedding with a silver shine, depending on how the light caught it. I shuddered, thinking of ways not to end up there. I was sure he used black to hide stains.

Against the wall was a headboard with hoops and hand-cuffs—or shackles. Neither made me comfortable.

Above the bed, adorned on the wall, were portraits of females in various erotic poses. I wondered how long they had to model for the artist to paint them. In between each female stood dogs with sinister features, salivating blood.

He adorned the bedside tables with a human skull and an animal skull with horns. Both held candles inside; emitting a relaxed ambiance. But there was nothing relaxing about this scene.

Something moved out of the corner of my eye and I glanced in that direction; Seth had removed his shoes and approached the cage. He unlocked it and opened the door.

He proffered his hand. "Come, Julia. I don't like you sitting in a dirty cage," he said, almost sticking his whole body inside the cage to reach me.

"No, thanks. It's safer to stay here than anywhere near you." I didn't know where that came from, but I was proud of myself for saying it. I was standing up for myself. If only I did it sooner, then I wouldn't have been in this mess in the first place.

"I promise not to hurt you. I only want to talk." His tone soft, almost gentle, like he was trying not to scare the bejeezus out of me. But it was too late for that. I was already afraid. And from what Os and Ossie had said about him, he was the worst demon of them all. I didn't know if I could trust him.

I narrowed my eyes; not trusting his words.

He stepped backward, leaving the cage door open, and sat on one of the large chairs at the foot of his bed.

"Please join me," he said, pointing at the empty chair beside him, "I only want to have a little chat." A glass materialized in his hand. He made a swirly gesture with his free index finger and the glass filled churning with honey-colored liquid and two ice blocks. "What's your poison? Champagne? Wine? Whiskey?" He snapped his fingers and a glass of each appeared on the table near the other chair.

Slowly, reluctantly, I stood up and left the safety of the dirty cage. If I was out of the cage, I had a better shot of escaping Seth. I doubted I could get far, but at least I had a fighting chance.

I sat in the empty chair but drank nothing. There could be poison in the glasses, making me amenable to his suggestions.

Seth sat comfortably in the chair, his enormous form only just fitting, sitting crossed legged. He balanced his glass on his knee, all the while staring at me.

I hated the way he made me feel; his dark gaze undressing me, layer for layer, caressing my skin. He needed to stop staring at me like I was dinner. I raised my head, giving him a deadpan stare.

Seth smirked. On any other guy, it would've been sexy, but not him. Even in his human form, his evil demeanor shone through like the sun. He was wicked to the bone. I didn't need to be a clairvoyant to know how dangerous he was.

"I must apologize for dragging you into the middle of things. But, it would seem you've stumbled upon a war between myself and Bill."

The moment he mentioned Bill's name, my jaw dropped, then quickly schooled my features.

Seth chuckled. Obviously, he'd seen my shocked expression and gave a curt nod. He sipped his drink, jerking his chin at the glasses before me. I shook my head. He shrugged.

"They are aware you've stumbled upon my lair and have asked for an exchange. Bill has something I've always wanted, and he wants you. But, you've bound yourself to my incubus and that just won't do. I'm waiting for my sigil master to remove it. Then I'll trade you for my item." His eyes darkened, blackness flooded his entire eyeball, then slowly receded, and his third eyelid moved.

For a second, I lost my words. I swallowed hard, my throat aching. As desperate as I was for something cold, I wouldn't drink anything Seth had offered. When I found my voice, I said, "What does he have?"

"Why? Do you think you can get it for me?"

I shrugged. "Maybe. I'd much rather get it for you than end up in his clutches."

"Okay, but remember, if you can't get it. I will use you in exchange for the item. Do we have a deal?" He held out his hand to shake on it.

Something told me not to touch his hand. It would seal my fate, condemning me to either party. I didn't want that. I would rather remain bound to an incubus for the rest of my life. At least I'd be orgasmically happy.

Bill and Seth would be the end of me.

Chapter Fourteen

OS

My brother was crazy. For a Demon Lord, that's the norm, but he was above and beyond.

Ossie stood back and admired his work. He'd drawn the blood sigils Victor had given him on the wall near Seth's chamber.

Since Julia bound herself to me, Ossie used my blood in order to find and get to her, while Bailey worked on the second sigil, which would release Julia from me and then we could get her back home.

Ossie closed his eyes and said the incantation. The sigils glowed red. Ossie's hands glowed with demonfire and the air popped.

The sigils ignited, burning a hole through the wall and into the cage.

"Why are you making a big-ass hole in the wall," I whispered. "It is now obvious someone was here." I pointed at the gaping hole before us.

"You're so dramatic for such a young demon. It's what Victor gave me."

"Well, it's terrible," — I grumbled, — "next time ask him if it could get us through walls without leaving evidence."

I rolled my eyes and neared the hole big enough for us to walk through. When a blast of power didn't strike us dead, I peered through the gap. The cage stood empty, with scuff marks on the floor. My eyes flitted towards the silken bed and then the rest of the chamber. It was unoccupied, except for us.

"Step aside, baby brother," Ossie said, pushing me out of the way and walked through the cage and farther into Seth's chamber.

I followed my brother and stopped near the two chairs with empty glasses on the table.

"Are the sigils supposed to do anything else?" I asked cautiously. I should've felt something if my brother had hurt Julia with the blood sigils, but I didn't. I couldn't recall seeing Julia with Seth when he left his chamber; she had to be somewhere nearby—Seth would never leave her alone for too long. He enjoyed keeping his toys safe. I shuddered at the thought of Julia being used by him.

"The sigils open a pathway to her," Ossie shrugged. "Victor said once we found her, I must complete the incantation to get us out of here. But I don't know if it will work for all of us."

"I can't believe you. You are not helping. Maybe you've just made it worse."

"This doesn't add up. Do you sense her like you did before?"

I relaxed my shoulders, closed my eyes, and sent my feelers out into the ether. I felt the cords attaching us and I felt her. Shaking my head, I said, "I feel her. It's as if she's sitting there," — I pointed at the closest seat, — "we just missed her. But we only saw Seth and one of his demons exit the chambers."

"Let's go. She isn't here," Ossie said, raising his hand with a red orb glowing in his palm. "Search!" He whispered into the orb, and it disappeared out of the newly made hole. As we exited the chamber, the red orb returned and hovered above the chair I pointed at.

I approached the chair. The closer I got, the skin on my forearms tingled as I felt her more. I leaned forward with an outstretched hand. I reached for thin air as if she was there, but there was nothing. Yet the orb continued to hover above the chair.

"I don't understand it—" A blast of black flames struck Ossie, cutting his words short. It sent him flying across the room as another flame ignited, aimed at me. I dove to the side, missing the energy blast by an inch.

I smelled burned hair and crispy flesh. Ossie moaned. He touched the fresh wound on his cheek, marked with Seth's black flame.

Seth and Julia materialized, cloaked by one of Seth's invisible spells.

"Boys, I wish you'd stop using Victor's sigils. They never work and I sense them a mile away." Seth stood, crossed the floor and proffered a hand. "Os, sit down," — he pointed at one of two new chairs that had appeared, — "we have much to discuss." He approached Ossie, who continued nursing his wounds. "Come, sit. Next time either of you tries something like this again, I won't be as gentle. You know I hate hurting you. But I will."

"You have a way of showing it," Ossie groaned, ignoring Seth's hand. He gave Seth a wide girth and sat beside me, still giving Seth the stink-eye.

Once we'd settled down, Seth explained what he

wanted. We knew Bill and couldn't stand the vampire; he was as shady as they came and we understood why Seth kicked him out of the nest.

Seth had a nest filled with various flavored demons and vampires, all doing various things for him on earth. They didn't get contracts like Victor's lackeys did, but they elicited destructive behavior; nudging a human with temptation was more rewarding than threatening them with violence.

Seth didn't go into detail about the item Bill had, only that it was a portrait above Bill's bed. He agreed to trade Julia for it. But she would rather retrieve it herself and hand it over; freeing herself from either party. And we agreed to help her get it. It was the least we could do for allowing Seth to capture her.

"Send us back. At the moment we're tied here——" I started.

"Easy," Seth said, snapping his fingers. "I'll be sending you directly to Bill's house. He rarely wakes during the day, so it should be fairly easy. And you may kill those who get in your way. They're Bill's people, so the less of his men around, the better for all," Seth added, making Julia shiver.

The weight I'd felt earlier, almost like chains holding me down, had lifted. But the invisible cord attached to Julia was still there; that ethereal rope moving from her chest to mine.

As much as I enjoyed having a stunning little mouse attached to me, I didn't want her tagging along for my nightly excursions. She wouldn't approve, and I needed daily sustenance; unless she was a willing participant— which I doubted—I had to sever the bond.

When we agreed to everything Seth wanted, he twirled his index finger, and the three of us teleported.

Chapter Fifteen

JULIA

It felt like my stomach was coming out of my mouth. I puked until there was nothing left. Then I dry-heaved to the point it felt like I was turning inside out.

"Easy," Os said, lightly rubbing my back. "It will pass."

The moment he touched me, my back tingled, sending sensual energy through my body and heat pooled between my legs.

"Please don't touch me," I mumbled, moving out of his grasp. "Every time you do," I glared at those crystal-colored eyes that threatened to drown me, "you make me feel things."

He grinned and stepped backwards, giving me space. "Sorry," he winked, "but that's just the kind of guy I am. I aim to please."

I stood up and shuddered. If Os had come any closer, I doubted I could contain myself. I wanted to get lost in his embrace and drown in his sexual energy.

When I stepped away from Os, he didn't seem to like that. Like I bruised his ego by creating distance between us.

He hissed, showing me his sharp teeth.

I flinched and stepped farther away.

"Take it easy, Os." Ossie pushed his brother away, stepping between us. "We don't have time for your games. We have work to do." He jerked his chin at the front door leading to Bill's place.

"Are we just going to enter?"

"He's down for the day, Julia. He won't know we're here," Os scowled at me.

I didn't know what was wrong with him, but I ignored his mood swing. "What if he has guards? I know there's one guy always with him."

"If anyone gets in our way, we end them, Julia. Now stay behind us," Ossie said, pushing me behind them.

I had nothing to say, so I kept quiet while I watched them do what they did best.

We crept up the porch steps and Os opened the front door. He morphed into his purple incubus form, sending waves of goosebumps across my body. I wanted to tell him to stop, but we needed to be quiet. And all I heard was my pulse thumping in my ears.

Bill's house was a mini mansion meant for the rich and disastrous. Every luxury item a slap in the face if one was from the poor part of town.

As we traversed up the stairs into the entrance hall, the smell of blood and organs assaulted my nostrils. I pinched my nose closed, but then I tasted the blood. A shudder ran through me as I imagined what Bill had gotten up to with humans he discarded so easily.

Silence filled the void. We stopped near a large curved staircase leading to the first floor, Bill's room. I paused, not wanting to go farther, but I had to, otherwise Seth would hand me over to Bill.

Ossie morphed into his enormous, dark, scaly self. His metallic scales shone in silvery blues, purples, and pinks, depending on how the light struck it. He was dangerously beautiful.

I'd been inside Bill's house with Desmond for parties, or when Desmond spoke privately with Bill while I waited with Bill's women. The conversation with his harem turned boring quickly. All they spoke about was how much they loved Bill. I suspected he had enthralled them and he enjoyed their words—it fed into his ego.

Usually Bill's house was a pleasant temperature; today I saw my breath in front of my face. I shivered, rubbing my arms. The hairs on the back of my neck stood on end. The darkness thick and suffocating. I didn't like this and needed some comfort.

Since Os was being a prick, I held Ossie's massive warm hand; which eased my nerves. His demonic form was twice my size and if I didn't know his personality, I would've been afraid for my life. He was just so imposing. But deep down, he was just a softie.

Before heading upstairs to the first floor, we first checked both sides of the staircase, ensuring there were no goons hiding somewhere. They had drawn the curtains, the open plan living area ominous, and the kitchen quiet.

Once we were content that no bad guys would jump out at us. We traversed up the carpeted stairs, heading towards the only room on the floor. The walls were painted black, with maroon luminaires and framed portraits adorned on the walls.

The house was eerily quiet, and I couldn't help but sense we were heading towards a trap. There was no way a vampire like Bill would allow us to walk inside. He always had someone watching during the day, yet today there was nobody. He was completely alone.

Before we entered the bedroom, I placed a hand on both brothers' shoulders. They glanced down at the same time, but Ossie shrugged as if to ask *what's wrong?*.

"What if it's a trap?" I whispered.

Os rolled his eyes.

I scowled at him.

"We might not win a fight against Seth, but we can fight Bill," Ossie said, turning around and headed inside the bedroom first.

We followed him inside the dark room; there wasn't even a sliver of sunlight shining through. I couldn't even see my hand in front of my face. I reached out for Ossie. The moment I touched him, electricity shot through my arm and I knew it was Os. Too nervous and scared to let go, I clung to him.

Os squeezed my hand, sending another jolt of sensual flames up my arm, and led me farther inside Bill's lair. The stench of blood stronger, and the air cooler.

When Os stopped, I slipped my arm through his and held tightly. Delectable vibrations came off him, making me squirm. I hated how he did that to me, but also relieved I wasn't here on my own.

In the thick blackness, I watched Ossie open his palm and a red orb glowed faintly, illuminating the bed. Bill lay face down with his dark hair covering his face, dead to the world. On the wall was the item; the painting.

I couldn't understand why Seth wanted a portrait of Bill. It was an intimate piece, yet it sounded as if Seth had wanted it for a long time.

The orb rose in the air while Ossie carefully removed the painting.

I held my breath the entire time it took us to descend the stairs and get outside Bill's house. I finally relaxed as we continued running down the street.

While we were inside the house, Ossie had somehow notified Bailey of our whereabouts. I still needed to ask her how she became involved with a Demon Lord and a direct line to him. She'd never spoken about him before, which left their whole situation puzzling.

I saw Bailey's silver Prius before I heard it. She was one of the most environmentally friendly witches I knew; she was the only witch friend I had but nobody was counting. The Prius idled as she waited for us at the corner two blocks down from Bill's residence.

"Hey hun," Bailey said as we hugged. "Are you okay?" she asked with concern in her voice and fine lines between her brows. "When Ossie told me what had happened, I felt terrible for leaving you—"

"It's okay," I said, still hugging her. There was no point in complaining. I'd messed up. It might not have happened if Bailey had helped me. But it's done. Now we needed to undo it so I could escape Desmond.

When Bailey stopped hugging, I had to let go, but I didn't want to. Reluctantly, I stepped back. The back of my throat ached as relief washed over me. Just knowing my friend was nearby soothed the tension between my shoulder blades. But there was no time to relax, we had to finish this.

"Let's go somewhere we can chat." She smiled, opened her car door, and climbed inside.

My heart was still trying to beat out my chest while the brothers seemed to take it in their stride. What we did seemed too easy, like they wanted us to take the portrait. I wanted to ask them about it, but Ossie was already telling Bailey what we did while Os seemed too calm.

I climbed into the backseat of Bailey's car with Os while Ossie sat in front.

Bailey drove into traffic at a leisurely speed.

I furrowed my brows as Ossie continued his conversation with Bailey, as if what we did meant nothing.

"Guys, I'm sorry, but how can you just continue—"

"What?" Ossie asked. He'd morphed back into his human form while we ran and arched an eyebrow.

"Don't you think it was all too easy? Like Bill wanted us to steal it?" I asked, widening my eyes and raising my eyebrows.

The brothers glanced at me like I'd sprouted horns while Bailey continued driving.

"Should I tell her?" Os said, staring at his brother.

Ossie nodded.

"It was easy because Seth made it easy. But we were prepared for anything. And besides, we've never trusted Seth or Bill," Os said beside me, patting my hand as if that would calm me—it didn't. Instant sparks shot through my hand and up my arm. I wanted to move my hand away, but it felt too nice. It was warm and soothing. "We know the reason Seth wants Bill's painting." He lifted the portrait from where he'd placed it on the floor of the vehicle and showed it to me. "Bill used to be part of Seth's nest and did a lot for him. Then one day he had enough and cut ties. Because Seth doesn't roam earth, and nobody could find Bill. It gave Bill the perfect opportunity to build his own empire. And from what I gather, Desmond has been part of that since the beginning."

I nodded slowly as my mind was trying to process the

information. I still didn't understand what he was getting at. "Okay, but I don't understand. And how do you know all this?"

"We've been part of Seth's nest from... well, from the beginning. And we know Bill." Os must've seen the lines between my brows deepen and added. "Let me explain. When Seth sired a fledgling, he had their portrait painted. It's not just any old painting. They painted each portrait with the life essence of that fledgling—especially vampires. Seth uses it to control them. If there's one cut, or manipulation of the portrait, it would cause the actual vampire to experience the injury or change." Os pointed at Bill's smugly painted face.

I scrunched my face. "I still don't get it."

Os's hands morphed into sharp black claws. He raised his hand and sliced the portrait on Bill's finger. Immediately blood pooled near the freshly chopped finger.

I gasped, finally understanding what it meant. "And Seth can use this painting to force Bill back into his nest? Or whatever he wants Bill to do."

The brothers grinned at me like I was a cat who caught the bird.

Chapter Sixteen

JULIA

We sat at a diner. The brothers ordered three meals each. Bailey wanted black coffee, and I ordered a burger and fries.

While Bailey went over spells from her tome and the brothers ate, I picked at my fries, deep in thought. I still couldn't believe we could enter Bill's house and take his portrait so easily. Nothing was ever easy. If it was, the world would be a happier place.

"What's on your mind, love," Os said with a wink.

"Ugh, please don't call me that," I groaned, and had a sip of my soda.

Os shrugged nonchalantly. "I'll be calling you that often, my dear," he chuckled.

"You wish."

"Honey, one taste of me and you'll beg for me to call you whatever I want." Os placed his palms on his chest and slowly moved down his hard body. His navy blue shirt outlined his muscles without looking like it was a size too small.

Bailey laughed beside me, pretending to read her spells.

Ossie choked on his food, then recovered quickly.

While Os stared at me like an apex predator would its victim, my neck heated as a blast of his luscious power smacked into me with such force, I did everything in my power not to squirm in my seat.

"Enough!" I threw my fry at Os and stood.

"Wait," Os said, grabbing my wrist. "I'll stop. Sit down." He let go of my wrist, raising both hands in surrender. "You're way uptight."

I groaned as I sat back down.

"Don't worry, I'll find something to reverse it," Bailey said as she hugged me from the side. "What you did was almost semi-permanent and a little tricky, especially since I'd already prepared it for Ossie to be bound to you. I still can't believe you made it work though," she said while turning a page in her tome. "Are you sure you don't have any witchy powers?"

"No," I said, shaking my head. "Why do you ask?"

"My spell shouldn't have worked if you messed up the order of the sentences and pronounced the Demon Lord's name incorrectly. Yet, you not only got it right, but you bound yourself to poor Os. Although I don't think he minds," she said, staring at Os. "And nice skin Os, very delicious. Even I would do you if I didn't prefer the company of women."

Os purred.

I rolled my eyes.

"I don't think I have any power." I picked up a fry and shoved it into my mouth. "I'm just glad I didn't bind myself to Seth. Could you imagine?" The table stilled, becoming eerily quiet. I glanced from one to the other while they stared at me with wide eyes. "What?"

Os and Ossie glanced nervously at each other, then back at me.

"What guys?"

"Nothing, but now that you say it. It's possible Seth already knew about you. That's why he came to Ossie's library. He knew when you arrived in the Underworld and was already searching for you. But why?" Behind Os's cool-blue eyes was a flicker of concern.

"What does it mean?" I whispered. "Am I in more trouble than we thought?"

Ossie shook his head. "Darling, if Seth wanted you dead, he would've done it already. Besides, once we give him the portrait and he brings Bill back to the Underworld, you'll be free. Then get you away from Desmond," Ossie said, glancing at Bailey and added, "And break the bond."

"Okay," I said, but nothing about this felt okay. I was missing something.

Chapter Seventeen

Bailey took us to her home, a quaint bungalow on the other side of town. It boasted two bedrooms, one bathroom, and an open plan living area and kitchen. It was small, yet comfortable.

This was the first time I'd met Bailey. She'd already indicated she preferred the company of women, but there was no sign of a partner living with her, or a partner at all. There were pictures of her and Julia on the wall. I wondered how close they really were or if the attraction was one sided. Or they were just friends, and I was hoping for a threesome. I snickered at the thought.

Julia had said neither Bill nor Desmond knew much about Bailey. She'd mentioned she had a roommate before she moved in with Desmond and that was the extent of their knowledge of Bailey. But knowing Bill, and his need to control everything, he might have looked a bit further into Bailey. I was still hopeful they didn't know where she lived. For now, we were safe.

After a lengthy discussion with Julia, I agreed with her.

At first, I had my reservations. I didn't want to think anything of it, but the more Julia spoke about it, the more I understood what she was getting at. Everything had been too easy. Julia should never have arrived in the Underworld, yet she did. She'd completely messed up the incantation, yet what she did was impossible. Not forgetting the fact that we had grabbed Bill's portrait with such ease.

Bill would come for us once he awoke. We were easier targets than Seth was. And since Bill never wanted to set foot in the Underworld again, he would rather slaughter us to get his portrait back. That's why we needed to give it to Seth as soon as possible.

Our next steps were to return the portrait and break the binding.

Ossie and I readied ourselves to return to the Underworld to give Seth the portrait, while Julia stayed with Bailey. I didn't like the idea of leaving her alone and hoped our bonds didn't hurt with distance between us but we had to try. By keeping Julia with Bailey, Seth couldn't reach her. But Desmond could still come after her. I didn't like either option but we had to finish this.

While Bailey and Ossie discussed the incantations Victor had given them to undo the binding, Julia was lying on the couch. She had just closed her eyes when I entered the living room.

I watched her; the steady rising and falling of her chest; the peaks of her supple breasts. Her mouth now slightly parted as she gave in to her exhaustion. The last couple of days had been difficult on her. She was only human, yet had gone through so much already. She didn't deserve any of it. I could tell Desmond had badly hurt her without knowing the details. Her need to hold my hand even though I repulsed her with my delicious power spoke volumes.

I stared fervently at her; it took little for my body to react to the female form, but Julia was different. Heat bloomed in my chest. The bulge in my pants grew bigger. As much as I wanted her in my bed, my need to protect her was greater.

Julia was a kind person, yet had fallen in with the wrong crowd. She had only known Desmond for less than a year, and he'd already messed with her life. Every time someone said Desmond's name, she'd flinch. I saw the bruises on her body and I'd gladly remove his arms first before killing him.

I sat on the coffee table, propped my elbows on my knees, and took her in. The delicate slope of her nose. Her thin yet defined lips; they were the perfect kissable shape. And when she smiled, her cheek dented slightly on one side with a cute dimple.

I felt my smile reach my eyes as I carelessly reached for her.

My stomach grumbled; my energy reserves almost depleted. Julia had pulled me back to the Underworld during my feeding and I was ravenous; I needed sustenance. And Julia was here. I wanted one tiny taste of her essence; so small she wouldn't notice.

My fingers brushed against her soft cheek. She stirred and turned onto her side, facing away from me. Her body dipped into the couch, highlighting her slender waist and the curve of her hips. Her ass wasn't large or small, just the right shape and softness. I wanted to bite that plump ass—softly.

I trailed my fingers down her spine. The sensation of the touch could feed me for hours, but I wanted more. I wanted a reaction from her. I wanted to show her what was possible if we were intimate. That she could have as much of me as she wanted. I palmed her ass and Julia moaned in her dream.

But this didn't feel right. Something told me not to do what I always did. I didn't want to feed on her essence while she slept. I hated being that demon—a thief in the night. She had to give herself willingly. I needed Julia to want me. She needed to be awake and offer herself to me.

Standing up from my position, I climbed onto the couch with Julia and wrapped my arm around her. I wanted to hold her. I didn't want to do anything that would cause distrust between us.

The bond we shared was like an invisible rope that tugged on my chest the farther we were from one another. But when I was near her like this, the tension eased the tightness in my ribs.

Her warm body heating my front a welcome sensation. I closed my eyes for a moment and enjoyed this little slice of heaven in my daily hell.

I awoke with a slap to the face. I jackknifed off the couch, landing with a thud on the floor. "Ow, what was that for?" I said, rubbing my cheek.

"What do you think you're doing?" Julia said, closing her top tightly around her body, hugging herself.

"Lying beside you. I was tired. I might be an incubus but I still sleep." I stood up and sat at the far end of the couch. "And you looked comfortable enough to sleep next to," I said with a wink.

"Argh," she complained and sat farther away from me without falling off the couch.

"Admit it, it felt nice," I said, remembering how I felt

curled up behind her; the heat from our bodies, the tightness around my chest easing, and I floated into a slumber.

Julia scowled at me, but her eyes gave her away. She felt something, too.

"Can you imagine how our senses would ignite if our skin touched?" I said with no hint of humor.

She remained quiet, but I heard her swallow.

I closed the distance and sat beside Julia, wrapping my arm around her shoulders, and pulled her closer. She unhooked my arm and pushed me away.

"I know what you're trying to do, Os. And the answer is no."

"What?" I grinned. "Can't I sit here."

"You can sit, you can't touch," she glowered at me.

I leaned forward. "What did you dream?" I asked, remembering her soft mewling sounds before I climbed in behind her. Although I barely touched her, I knew I struck something within her.

She narrowed her eyes, her expression filled with suspicion as she recalled her dream.

"You want me, don't you?" I breathed near the shell of her ear and watched all the little hairs on her neck rise, making me smile. "I want you too."

"Ugh," she scooted to the other side of the couch and folded her arms.

Not wanting to make her any more uncomfortable, even though I sensed her desire. Perhaps the way to her heart was through her mind. If we didn't touch now, then we'd talk; get to know each other. Perhaps changing the subject would stop her squirming, even though I enjoyed making her uncomfortable. There was nothing wrong with lighting a small fire within her. It was good for her soul. And besides, how could I deny such a beautiful face.

"You'll come around, my little mouse. Anyway, let's talk about something else." She didn't respond. "Do you have questions you want to ask? You know, since I'm a demon and all that." I waved a hand in the air.

Her eyes flitted to the ceiling. I sensed the cogs in her mind spinning. Yep, this was how to get through to her; to smash the walls Desmond had forced upon her.

"How old are you?"

"A demon never gives his age away. But I can tell you I've been around for a very long time."

Julia turned sideways, bringing her left leg onto the couch, staring at me. "And... well, go on."

"You want to hear about me?"

She nodded enthusiastically.

I didn't tell her my exact age, more the era I was born. That Ossie and I were twins, and our kind mother had fallen pregnant and birthed us, and left us when we were still young. We didn't know who she was but there was a lost diary that explained everything.

I didn't tell her who our father was. Nobody knew. Julia would be in danger if she found out, and I couldn't risk it.

And even though Ossie and I were different kinds of demons, we were both Demon Lords. But because Ossie was first born, they widely feared his flavor demon, while they lusted after mine. Who wouldn't want thrills and delicious vibrations in their life? I brought happiness, while Ossie brought destruction and fear. But he never used that part of him and preferred remaining in his library.

I explained how I preferred to remain in my demon form and fed on the essence of the willing. I may have nudged them along, but I never forced myself on them. A pervert, I was not.

"That's amazing," Julia beamed. "There's so much I

don't know about the supernatural world, even though I've been friends with Bailey. But what I found interesting was that there's so many kinds of demons."

"Yep, and we have our own way of dying. That's why it's best if your enemy doesn't know everything. Or it could destroy us."

"And that's why you won't tell me when you were born or who your father is?"

I nodded.

Since we were bonding, I explained how someone could use the name of a demon against them, so it was imperative she didn't repeat my or Ossie's name to anyone. She tensed at my confession and thanked me. I trusted her with that information and with my name. She understood how evil humans could be and she wasn't the type who enjoyed inflicting pain on others.

When silence filled the space between us. She cocked her head to the side, considering me as she thought of her next round of questions.

"And you've never found yourself someone you'd want to keep around?" she asked with innocence shining in her eyes.

"If I fed on the same woman every day, I'd kill her; draining her life essence is not a pleasant way to die."

Julia gasped, covering her mouth.

"That's why it must be someone different every night."

"Can incubi mate with one woman and then feed on others?"

"We can." My smile reached my eyes.

"But you don't have one?"

"Nope."

"Why not?"

"Dunno. Maybe I haven't met her yet. Or she hasn't been born." I winked and watched her blush.

She was quiet for a moment. I could tell the wheels inside her head were spinning; there were multiple questions she wanted to ask but didn't know which to ask first.

"Would your mate turn purple too?"

"She would become a succubus and yes, she'd turn purple, have a tail and sexy horns." I licked my lips.

Something flashed in Julia's eyes that warmed my heart. But I didn't want to take it out of context or embarrass her further by asking her questions. She wanted to know about me.

"Are you ready?" Ossie entered the living area in his demon form. He almost doubled over to enter the room and stood hunched or he'd hit the ceiling. "I want to get this over with."

Chapter Eighteen

OS

I rounded my shoulders as we traversed the hallways of the Underworld. My shoulder muscles spasmed as I held onto the portrait.

In demon form, I had no hair, but something pricked at my skin. A nervousness I previously ignored now in full force.

"I don't like this," Ossie said beside me. In these hallways, he stood his full length. His power beat against me as he, too, sensed something.

"Seth is setting us up."

"Yep," Ossie said as we entered Seth's chamber. "And we're about to find out how."

Seth's chamber was empty, yet his power lingered. Either he was nearby or we'd just missed him.

I placed the portrait on a chair and sat on the other chair. Ossie remained standing, leaning against the wall and folded his arms.

The sound of footsteps echoed down the hallway, then Seth materialized through the wall with a broad smile. "Just in time, boys." He ignored us as he approached the portrait. "Finally," he said, picking it up and crossed the floor to the other side. He raised his palm, and the wall dissolved, leading into his private safe.

I arched an eyebrow, glancing in Ossie's direction. He nodded in understanding. I couldn't believe Seth opened his private safe with us in full view of the contents. We had never seen it before. Ever. We should remain guarded, especially now that we'd been privy to what was inside.

The safe held multiple portraits, including ours, along with precious items he'd collected over the ages or had stolen from Victor.

Ossie pushed away from the wall, heading towards the private safe. I stood up and caught his elbow, shaking my head.

"Don't do it. You won't like what's in there," I whispered.

"You know I have to," Ossie said, yanking his elbow out of my hand.

I followed closely behind him, but he was so large and bulky I had to peer around him to see.

Seth settled the portrait of Bill on a shelf, chuckled at the cut I'd made when I showed Julia what it meant to possess such a painting.

"Did Bill do anything when you cut off his finger? I see he hasn't replaced it yet, it's still severed." Seth exited his safe, and it closed behind him.

"No, it was frightfully easy to access his house and grab it. It was almost too easy."

Seth glanced between Ossie and me, the lines between his brows deepening. "I only facilitated access to his house. Did he have no guards?"

"Nope," I said, leaning against his desk.

"Anyway, he'd never come down here, so I'd love to know what he'll do next," Seth grinned and sat behind his desk, his chair creaking as he sat back. "Right, give this to Bailey," he said, handing Ossie a piece of paper.

Ossie's confusion matched my own. I stood up and stepped away from his desk and considered Seth.

"Boys, don't look so worried. Yes, I knew about Bill. Yes, I facilitated poor Julia's trip down here. You should know I'm the rightful Underworld keeper, even if my brother rules over it. No-one gets down here without my knowledge."

Ossie glanced at the incantations and nodded his approval. "It might work."

"I didn't expect her messing up the order or saying Os's name, but I developed it so that she bound herself to either of you no matter what she did."

"But Bailey and I wrote it together," Ossie said. His tone deeper and unsure. "How did you—"

"You found it from a book in your library, didn't you?"

Ossie nodded slowly.

"Well, there you go…," Seth said, raising his hand as if to say it was him. "The power of suggestion hurt no-one." He flew up in one swift motion, neatening his vest and fastened the buttons. Today he wore a double-breasted suit —he never wore suits.

"Are you meeting the queen?" I asked with humor laced in my question.

"You know I don't kiss and tell."

"What should we do if Bill asks for his portrait back?"

"He won't be around for much longer. I will end him after my meeting," Seth said, moving towards the door. "Wait here until I return. When I'm done, I need you to distribute what's left of the portrait to Bill's subordinates.

They need to know I'm King. Once that's done, get back to Julia and remove the binding. I'm sure her boyfriend will be after her, so she'll need protecting. And while you're there, don't get dead. I need your help with other business," he said and disappeared.

Ossie and I stared at each other. This was going to cause a war between us and Bill.

Chapter Nineteen

JULIA

I didn't like the way Os made me feel—which was everything—I felt his lust, desire, kindness, and pity.

I'd just fallen asleep when I dreamed of him and it felt so good. Then, when I felt him climb on the couch behind me, my heart rate sped up. Hope filled my veins and I didn't like those feelings either. He did this with a different woman every day. I was just some girl he wanted to feed on.

I'd gone through enough with Desmond, and now I finally had the courage to move forward. The last thing I needed in my life was to be used by an incubus.

I was hopeful of the idea of Os or someone like him, but at the same time, I needed to be on my own for a while to heal and to figure out what I wanted.

Desmond would force his wants and needs onto me. Now that I was almost free, I wanted to do my own thing.

I had to keep my distance. Not touching Os cleared my head. Then, when our conversation flowed, I enjoyed learning more about him. And he almost sounded human.

Our exchange was casual, although he tried to flirt with me every chance he got.

It was fun.

When Os left with Ossie for the Underworld, I felt the invisible rope tying us together tug on my chest but it didn't hurt. I was grateful the distance didn't cause pain or put additional strain on us.

I wanted to see what Bailey was up to and found her in her spare bedroom. She sat cross-legged on the floor with her tome and the incantations Victor had given Ossie. She kept shaking her head and crossed out words, then rewrote them.

"Something wrong?" I asked, sitting beside her.

She sighed. "The spell shouldn't have worked. It had to be said in order and the words pronounced correctly." She shook her head again, then pinched the bridge of her nose. "I don't understand it. And if I look at Victor's incantation to break the bond and my spell books, I don't think either will work."

I closed her books, picked up the piece of paper and placed it on top of the book along with her pencil.

"Leave it for now. Let's make some tea, or pour shots of tequila," I grinned. "I'm tired of thinking. Come. Let's have some girl-time." I stood up and reached for her hands.

Bailey grabbed my hands and I pulled her to her feet.

"I like this Julia. I haven't seen her in ages." Bailey wrapped her arm around my shoulders as we headed towards the kitchen.

"Yeah, I hid away for a while. And in a couple of hours, Desmond will have me. Bill will torture, then kill me. Os and Ossie might break the bond. And after that, who knows? But right now. All I want is to drink with my best friend and not think about any of that."

The bottle of tequila sat at the half-way mark. Bailey was on the floor, giggling. I was laughing and pointing at her sitting on the floor.

Bailey had tried to stand to wash her hands, but her foot caught on the leg of the chair and she crashed to the floor with a painful thump.

Tears streamed down my face. Bailey kept wiping her eyes. Her falling wasn't that amusing, yet it was.

Her cheeks glowed, and I wiped my forehead. It wasn't a warm evening; it was just the alcohol making us hot; and all the laughing made it worse.

"Ah man, that was funny," I said, proffering a hand to help her up.

"Nah, I'm good." Bailey used the kitchen counter to climb to her feet and then washed her hands. "This was fun, Jules."

"Yep, it was." I sighed. "You got food?" I rubbed my stomach for effect. I'd been in the Underworld for at least twenty-four hours without eating and had only nibbled on some fries at the diner; I was famished. It amazed me I hadn't reacted badly to the alcohol on an empty stomach.

"Pizza?"

My mouth watered. "Yesss, with extra cheese."

I had fun, but I didn't want to wake tomorrow morning with a hangover. That was the last thing I needed. While Bailey ordered a couple of pizzas with extra cheese, I filled the kettle and switched it on. I'd lived with Bailey before moving in with Desmond, and she kept everything the way it was before I'd moved out.

Bailey entered the kitchen as I finished preparing the tea.

"Are we done drinking?"

"I am." I brought the warm tea to my lips for a sip. Delicious. "But you're welcome to carry on. I don't think I can stomach anymore."

"Nah, I don't enjoy drinking alone. This is perfect. And it saves us from dying tomorrow morning."

"Exactly."

Bailey glanced at the clock. "The pizzas should arrive in fifteen."

With the laughter gone, reality seeped in again. I glanced down at my dirty clothing and was sure I smelled awful. I was sure Bailey had clothing I could borrow, but I wanted my stuff; my brush, my deodorant, my underwear. There was something comforting about using my belongings and wanted to fetch my things from Desmond's house.

"What's on your mind?"

"Just thinking."

"About?"

"All my stuff. I need a shower, brush my teeth, put clean clothing on."

"You know you can use anything of mine." She offered.

"I know—"

"But you want your stuff. I get it."

"Do you think Desmond burned my things?"

She shrugged.

"If Bill knew I asked for help, he'd definitely tell Desmond. And if Desmond knew what I was up to, it's possible."

"Should we see if anyone is home?" She wiggled her eyebrows.

"As in break-in?"

"Why not? Do you have your keys?"

"No, he took them."

"I can always charm our way inside."

"But what if he's there?"

"What if he's not? Grab all your stuff, come back here and enjoy a nice hot shower."

"And remind me to take my photo album. It's the only photos I have of my folks." My parents had died a few years ago, and I only had those copies. There were other photos but I'd lost them when I had to move.

"And the jewelry your mom left you."

"Hmm," I sipped my tea, "I'd only been gone a short while and doubt Desmond had time to do anything."

"We should go check."

I nodded.

———

I burped pizza with the aftertaste of tequila and shuddered. The combination left me nauseated and was glad I stopped drinking when we did, otherwise I'd be crawling.

"Ew, that was disgusting," Bailey whispered as we walked in a crouched gait towards Desmond's house.

"Sorry," I breathed, fighting another burp.

I assumed Desmond wasn't home because darkness surrounded the house; the light from the street our only salvation. Hopefully, he was with Bill somewhere far away.

I followed Bailey towards the back of the house where nobody would see us sneak inside.

Bailey climbed the stairs, kicked the top step, tripping herself, and falling on her hands and knees with a loud thud. She bubbled with hysterics while I bit down on my knuckles, trying not to alert the neighbors to our childish behavior. Tears streamed down my cheeks as I tried to control my laughter, but it was funny how she'd landed. In the dim moonlight, Bailey looked like a crab with her ass in the air.

"Oh man, that hurt," she said softly, "ow," she cried, moving onto her butt and rubbed her knees. "I'm going to have the biggest bruises tomorrow."

"You're clumsy," I guffawed.

"Shh!" She brought her finger to her lips. "You'll wake the neighbors." Slowly, she climbed to her feet, limped and when she reached the back door, held out her hand. A faint ball of light glowed in her palm. She waved her other hand near the door handle and it clicked open.

"Just like that?"

"Exactly like that."

"You're good."

"I know," Bailey sang and opened the door.

A blast of stale air hit our faces. I coughed into my hands and waved dust particles away. The kitchen in the exact way I'd left it.

"It doesn't look like he's been home since you left," Bailey said, holding the glowing orb higher for my benefit.

"I was only gone for a day——"

"Three days," she corrected.

"Three? It doesn't feel that long."

"Time is different down there. It's slower," she offered. "Come," — she grabbed my elbow, — "let's get your things and go."

We entered the bedroom and that too was in the exact same way I had left it. I opened my closet, reached for my bag, and started packing.

"My photo album is in the basket on the coffee table in the parlor." I pointed towards the area.

"Sure, and here," Bailey said, leaving one of her glow thingies by me.

I packed as much clothing as I could fit in my bags, and filled my cosmetics bag with my toiletries from the bathroom.

If Desmond didn't think I was coming home before, he'd know now. The bedroom looked pillaged with open drawers and closet doors, while the bathroom void of my things.

When I was happy I'd taken everything I needed. I walked through the house one last time.

Bailey carried my photo album, then stopped in the living room. My circle of salt ruined by scuff marks on the floor. The knife slashed through the couch. And the walls littered with holes; I suspected Desmond had slammed his fists into the walls after he entered his house, finding me missing.

"He must know you helped me," I said, glancing at the destroyed scene. I was on a buzz when we were out back and when Bailey had fallen, but after seeing what Des had done, I was wide awake and fear crept in. "I wonder where he is." I picked up my cellphone; the screen cracked, and it didn't switch on. I removed the SIM card, pocketing it.

"I'll get you a new one," Bailey said, bringing me in for a sideways hug. "Come, let's get out of here."

Once we were back at Bailey's place, I packed my things in her spare bedroom. She had kept it the way I'd left it when I first moved out. I doubted she wanted a new room-mate in case I came back.

I owned little; in my bag I had clothing, the photo album, and my jewelry box. My parents had died in a car accident three years ago with too much debt against their name. The money they'd left me had all gone to paying their bills. At least they did not leave me with needing to pay with my money. I moved out of the house they had rented and moved in with Bailey.

I'd known Bailey for years and loved her like a sister, even though she had shown she wanted more than friendship. After I broke her heart gently, I promised never to push her away because she was still my best friend.

"All settled in?" Bailey asked, sticking her head between the open door and door frame.

"Yeah, all done. Luckily I had little."

"Stay for as long as you like." She entered and sat beside me on the bed.

"Thanks, you're a good friend."

There was a quick display of discomfort. I didn't think she knew I saw it, but I did. She wrapped her arm around my shoulder and hugged me.

"Anytime, you know that. And here," she handed me a set of keys, "it's your old set."

I squeezed Smurfette, and she only let out stale air. "And the same keyring."

"There's no way I could give it to someone else," Bailey said with a warm smile.

"Do you mind if I shower quickly?" I said, not liking the feel of grime on my body.

"Go right ahead." She stood up, turned to say something, then stopped.

"What's wrong?" I asked.

"Nothing. You remember where the towels are?"

I nodded, not understanding what that was about, but ignored it. I had too much on my mind at the moment and would address Bailey's concerns when all this was over.

I opened the hallway closet and pulled out two towels. Bailey had swapped the items on the shelves around since last I remembered; the towels were now on the bottom shelf.

She filled the other shelves with boxes, linen, and old crockery; a mishmash of items belonging nowhere, yet needed one day.

I undressed and climbed into the shower, opened the hot tap on high until my skin burned. It was a relief washing the gunk off my body. I washed my hair twice and rinsed with lukewarm water.

My body ached, but at least I was clean. My thoughts wandered to the events of the week and decided I should write a book about my experience if I survived Desmond. I chuckled at the thought.

Seth would smite me into one of his chambers and keep it locked if I ever wrote about him. I'd seen his natural and human form; both equally frightening. Not forgetting the Demon Lord brothers; and Os with his sensual power. I shuddered as I dried my legs. Waves of gooseflesh swept across my skin.

An uneasiness slid down my spine, like a scalpel slicing my skin. I stood upright and glanced around. It felt as though someone was watching me. The bathroom window stood ajar. The bathroom filled with steam. I wiped the mirror, waiting for a demon to appear in the reflection, but there was nothing. It was just my imagination. Only I still felt someone watching me.

Not wanting to give them a strip show, I pulled the towel tighter around my body and dashed to my room. The hallway was dark and quiet. Bailey's bedroom door was closed. The open-plan living area and kitchen dark with only one light on in the kitchen. A chill ran through my body. I entered my room and slammed the door closed.

I didn't understand it, but it left me on edge. Dressing quickly, I didn't dry properly, and the clothing stuck to my damp body. I towel dried my hair, not bothering to blow-dry it.

Bailey's door creaked open. The bathroom door squeaked closed. Followed by the shower running.

Not knowing why, but something told me to go into Bailey's bedroom.

Carefully, I opened my bedroom door. My pulse swished in my ears, my heart thumped in my ribs. I tip-toed across the hallway and opened her bedroom door. Remembering it squeaked, I partially opened it.

Sticking my head inside; the first thing I saw was her unmade bed. Even back then, she never made it. She'd just climb into the mess from the previous night and sleep.

I surveyed the area; pictures torn from her walls, remnants of the corners still there. I furrowed my brows, not remembering what pictures, and stepped farther inside her room. Her door creaked. I white knuckled the door to stop it from sounding. The shower continued. She hadn't heard.

I glanced at the other side of the room; smaller pictures stuck at odd angles. Red candles blazing. Black candles melted. Wax on the tiled floor. I smelled wick and something coppery. The shower switched off. My heart started pounding. Not wanting to get caught. I tiptoed towards my bedroom, shutting the door as the bathroom door opened.

I switched off the bedroom light and when I closed my eyes, Bailey's room came into my mind. It was only candles burning in Bailey's room. There was nothing sinister. I had nothing to worry about. Bailey was a good witch. I'd never known her to hurt anyone. Not even her clients victims got hurt. Nothing was permanent. It was only my imagination.

After what felt like minutes, exhaustion finally took over. I would handle my issues tomorrow.

Chapter Twenty

OS

We barely moved when Seth returned. His suit now torn and missing buttons. Ossie and I stared at him; his expression nondescript. His power swarmed us like a beating drum ready to explode.

"Come!" He barked and went to his safe. He placed his palm on the wall again and it opened. "Don't just stand there, come inside."

Ossie and I shared a nervous glance and followed.

"With Bill gone, you can handle his human. Victor refused to give me his life-contract to aid you in destroying him," he said, waving his hands near his body as if to say Victor was the one who had ruined his suit. "The sooner you handle him, the better for Julia... and us."

If I didn't know Seth, I'd never have guessed he cared for Julia's life. But I supposed Desmond could become a potential threat if not destroyed soon after Bill. But the fact that he'd mentioned Julia's name made me wonder.

It was strange entering Seth's large safe. It smelled of

stale air, smoke, and ink. Inside were jewels, gold crowns, gold bars, various swords, amulets, and portraits of those part of his nest. In a glass cabinet were various unknown trinkets with an intricate lock securing them.

I didn't see my or Ossie's portraits and hoped Seth had tucked them away safely, or right at the bottom of the pile.

Adorned on the wall were portraits of Seth, a woman, and another man. I'd never seen them before and thought best not to ask. When I glanced at Seth, a fine haze surrounded him as if too hot for the cold air. He grunted as he stalked the portrait, his hands bunched into fists.

Seth reached for Bill's portrait, yanked it down and his hand morphed into sharp black claws. He stabbed the painting near Bill's head and raked down. His claws sliced through Bill's face in two parts and his body savagely cut into four streams.

My arms pebbled.

Ossie shuddered.

If we were near Bill, we'd see his body cut into parts and since he was a vampire, the one cut had perforated his heart, rendering him true-dead.

The portrait now in streams and bloody, Seth lifted it and hung it on the wall again. We watched it bleed. Guts spilled. Eye balls popped with pus. The lifelike portrait of Bill now ruined.

"There!" Seth beamed. "Doesn't that look better?"

Ossie and I nodded.

"Is Desmond a blood-servant to Bill?" I asked, curious as to the nature of their relationship and if Desmond was a blood-servant, it could make our jobs difficult.

"That he is," Seth answered, wiping his claws clean on a cloth.

"Won't he feel his master's passing?"

"He will, that's why he needs to be managed now."

I didn't like that. By feeling his master's passing could enrage him and go after Julia sooner. We had to get to her now.

Chapter Twenty-One

JULIA

I awoke with a start. Something heavy fell with a loud thud, followed by swearing. Bailey cried out, sounds of hard stomping, then bouts of laughter.

I climbed out of bed wondering what had happened to elicit such a response from her with a smile creeping up my face.

I knocked on her bedroom door. She opened the door with a swish—no creaking sounds—wearing a smile, but her eyes screamed pain.

"Hey, morning," she said, opening the door wider.

"Morning, is everything okay?" I giggled.

"Yeah," she said and limped to her bed. "I hit my toe on the foot of my bed when I avoided standing on the book." She picked up the book and threw it on her bed.

I glanced around the room, and it looked the same as last night. Even the strange candles on the table. My imagination ran away with me last night; there was nothing sinister going on. Perhaps I was just tired.

"What's with those?" I pointed at the candles. Being

curious, I still wanted to know what she was doing with the strange candles.

"Just something I buy to help me sleep. The aroma is more candle than scent, but it kills all other scents. Remember all the headaches I used to get?" I nodded. "I don't get them anymore since I light those every evening."

I understood where she was coming from. When I stayed here, her headaches were so bad she had to drink pain medication then sleep directly afterwards.

"I'm glad you found something that helps. And no medication?"

"Nope, no meds needed."

"Good." I sat on the bed beside her; silence filling the space between us. "Have you heard from Ossie, maybe?"

"Oh yeah, he sent me a message," — she tapped the side of her head, — "and Seth destroyed Bill's portrait and they'll be right up—"

Speak of the devils and they would arrive. Pounding started on the front door, cutting Bailey's words short. She wiggled her eyebrows and stuffed her feet inside fluffy devil slippers. I giggled at her choice of shoes.

Ossie and Os stood outside, in human form, both wearing matching sunglasses, snug white t-shirts and faded blue jeans. Their hair was neat and off their faces, freshly shaved, and charming smiles. They looked like a couple of models on a photo shoot. Os wore sandals and Ossie sneakers. They smelled of aftershave and male; very male with hints of sweat.

It was warm outside and scorching inside the house, even though the air conditioner was on. My clothing felt tight as I raked my eyes up and down their bodies. The sight of them even left Bailey blushing.

"You guys look like you dropped out of someone's wet

dream," Bailey said and swept her hand to the side so they could enter.

Ossie chuckled. The low rumbling sound struck my core. When Os entered, he peered at me over his sunglasses. His blue eyes sparkled with humor.

"I hope you missed me," Os said, slithering a hand behind my back and kissed my cheek.

My skin tingled where he touched, and I stared dumb-struck with lust.

"How did it go?" I said when I found my voice.

Os sat on the couch and patted the seat beside him. "Sit with me and I'll tell you all about it."

I arched an eyebrow and cocked out my hip.

He patted the seat again.

"Fine," I grumbled and sat beside him.

Os explained what had happened with the painting. And next they had to deal with Desmond. I understood what he meant, but it still made me uncomfortable.

"What do you think he'll do when he finds out Bill's dead?"

"That's why we need to find him quickly," Ossie said, pushing Bailey to one of her kitchen chairs so she could sit, then he sat beside her. I was curious whether Ossie knew of Bailey's inclination towards the fairer sex, especially since every time I saw them together he was always touching her or getting her attention. "When he finds out we destroyed Bill, he might do something foolish," he said, staring at me.

"Yeah, like round up Bill's fledglings and have one of them turn him," Os added.

"Really?" I asked. I doubted Desmond wanted to be a vampire, but then again, he always surprised me.

"Sure, you know Desmond is a blood-slave, don't you?" Os said. I nodded. "By being Bill's blood-slave, Desmond can live as long as Bill needs him; and typical vampire, they hardly change their blood-servant into a vampire. They'd much rather keep their blood supply flowing than add hungry mouths to feed. Once Desmond realizes Bill's demise, he'll ask to be turned. They all do."

I shuddered. I'd seen Desmond and Bill exchange blood in his nightclub and the art gallery, but I never wanted a taste, nor had I given blood to any vampire or supernatural. I snickered at the thought of being a 'blood virgin', but was definitely not a virgin in the bedroom. My eyes slowly drifted to Os, who sat beside me all male, and very yummy. Then, as if an ice cold bucket of water splashed against me when I thought… demon.

"But wait," I started. "I thought fledglings died when someone destroyed their master?"

Os nodded. "If the fledglings are powerful enough, they can live through it. Then they'll need to find a new blood master willing to take them."

"Unless Desmond wants to take that role."

"No vampire will change a human and then serve him," Os shook his head, "it would be suicide. It's like admitting you're the weaker vampire. They'd rather kill him."

"If I know Seth, he's already linked Bill's fledglings to him," Os said.

"Speaking of which. We're heading to his house but wanted to stop by to ensure you were okay?" Ossie said, breaking my reverie.

"He wasn't at home last night—"

"You went to his home?" Os asked. His tone filled with rage.

"I wanted to shower. But that's not what I'm getting at. He's probably at the nightclub or art gallery."

"Come, Ossie. Let's go."

"No, we're coming with." I stood up and walked towards my bedroom. "Give us five minutes to get dressed, then we can all go together."

Os groaned, but they waited.

Bailey's Prius purred silently as we drove to the first venue. Ossie sat in the passenger seat while Os and I sat in the back. Nobody spoke as we anxiously stared out the window. Bailey changed the music often, as though she too sensed our apprehension.

We drove past the nightclub, and it was eerily quiet; no cars out front, and the building dark. I wasn't up to going inside and doubted anyone was there; if there was, a light would be on.

In all the time I'd been with Desmond, I'd only been to the art gallery once to fetch him. I wasn't allowed inside and had to wait outside with the car idling like a cab driver.

Bailey parked near the entrance to the art gallery. I rolled my eyes at the name, *'Bill's Fine Art'*. The vampire was completely in love with himself. There was nothing fine about forgery. I didn't tell the others what I'd seen, as I didn't think it was necessary since Seth had destroyed Bill.

We climbed out of Bailey's car and approached the entrance. Ossie pulled on the doors and they clicked open. His eyebrows shot up, not expecting unlocked doors, and as we entered, a chilly breeze made me shudder.

"Where are all Bill's people?" I whispered near Os's shoulder.

"Not sure. But the possibility of them waiting some- where is high."

The art gallery had wide open spaces with walls that rose half-way to the ceiling. Adorned on the walls were portraits, some I'd seen in the forgery document.

The sun had set and splashed bright orange and red light across the eggshell walls. Another chill ran through me and I glanced over my shoulder, but there was nothing there.

Ossie flinched and shuddered. He doubled in size and his scales flowed over his body like fur, followed by the metal sound when the scales set in place.

Ossie's behavior fueled Os's change, and he shifted into his purply demon form. His power struck my side, causing waves of gooseflesh to caress my skin.

"What are you going to do? Love them to death?" I teased.

"Honey," — Os purred near the shell of my ear, — "you haven't felt my claws or teeth yet." Os snapped his jaw open and closed. He laughed when he saw my expression. I was sure I looked as scared as I felt.

Os's power confused me; one moment it's warm and fuzzy, the next I was ready to bolt.

The sound of metal clanking on the floor echoed in the large open space, and we froze. Our heads turned at once in that direction, then we approached. Os and Ossie went first, then Bailey, while I brought up the rear.

Ossie raised his large hand. A red orb glowed, and he whispered to it. The orb disappeared and returned. Ossie nodded, and the orb dissolved into his palm. "Vampire," he growled as we reached the doorjamb.

Bailey's hands glowed with her power and jealousy engulfed me for being the only non-magical person here. I even felt Os's power, albeit sensual.

Once we entered the kitchen, we came across a body on the floor; some poor soul had entered at the wrong time. One of Bill's men was still sucking on his neck.

Ossie threw a black orb in the vampire's direction, blasting him off the corpse and into the window, shattering it and burning the vampire when the half-sun slammed into him. Ash and burned flesh wafted in the air as I waved particles away.

"Ugh, that was gross," I said and exited the kitchen. Visions of the man's mutilated body on the floor flooded my mind. "There's nobody else here. I wonder where Desmond is." I mumbled to myself as I walked towards the entrance. The art gallery was empty. Desmond wasn't here or at the nightclub. "Either he's at Bill's house or back at his house," I said when I heard the others' footsteps behind me.

"Let's try Bill's place first," Os said, wrapping an arm around my shoulder. His purple skin was smooth as he closed the distance between us. He still smelled the same; aftershave, male, with an extra something... pepper, maybe. "You okay, darling?" he asked. "You look a little pale."

"I'm fine, just a little grossed out."

"Relax in my embrace. I got you." He brought me close enough to touch his side with mine. I felt uncomfortable with my arm hitting his leg, so I wrapped it around his waist. He purred. I held on; his skin silky smooth to my touch.

I flinched when something wrapped around my ankle; Os's tail. I grinned as I walked, then when I glanced up at him, he stared with fire burning in his eyes. Tiny flames of desire forced me to swallow hard.

When Ossie spoke, the flames died down. Os squeezed my shoulder but didn't let go.

"Let's go to Bill's house. Afterwards, we must find Bill's vampires. Perhaps they know his whereabouts. Let's try the club when they open," Ossie said as he brushed past us and exited.

Chapter Twenty-Two

OS

Ossie and I had to change back into human form while we rode in the tiny vehicle; no way could it accommodate Ossie's massive build; he'd break Bailey's car.

The trip to Bill's house was quick and although I had shifted into my human form, my tail kept hold of Julia's ankle. It's as if it had a mind of its own—I wasn't doing it.

Julia sat in the middle of the backseat, a smidge closer to me. I watched as the streetlights blurred past, shining on her face and highlighting her stunningly dainty features. Then, the shadows devoured her once more as the car moved past.

My tail tightened its hold on her. She didn't stir. I hoped it was comforting to have me holding onto her like it was for me. When she didn't swat me away, I took it as a good sign.

I glanced down her arm, at her hand pressing into the seat, her fingers spread out. I reached for her hand as the imaginary rope pulled us closer. The moment we touched, she glanced my way. She smiled slightly, genuinely, and my chest ached. Warmth flooded my system from head to toe.

I pulled her hand into mine, and she didn't resist. She

squeezed my hand reassuringly. I didn't know if it was for her sake or mine, but I liked it.

"Do you know I haven't been using any of my incubus powers on you?" I said, telling the truth. I hadn't had the need to. Even when she lay on the couch, I didn't push any of my power into her. She just seemed to react to my touch naturally.

She laughed like she didn't believe me.

"I swear, scout's honor." I raised two fingers.

"Were you even a scout?"

"Of course not. I'm a demon," I grinned.

"You serious?"

"As a corpse."

The lines between her pretty eyes deepened. "You're telling the truth."

"I didn't want to use my power," — I raised one shoulder nonchalantly, — "you weren't someone I wanted to feed off of like I usually did. Terrible things were happening around you. It would be awful of me to take advantage. And besides, the essence of those stressed is bitter and doesn't fill me. I need a cheerful person to fill me and you haven't been happy. But I'll be honest, I felt something while you slept on the couch."

She closed the gap, her knee touching mine. "Then what have I been feeling each time we touch?"

"You mean the electrical current shooting through us?" She nodded. "That's us, baby, that's all us."

"You're lying," she guffawed.

"Or it's the binding. Whatever it is, I don't think I'm ready to let go just yet." I admitted. The words caught me off guard, but it was out in the open. No way I could take them back. She already heard.

"What do you mean?" Julia asked. Her head was so close to mine if I leaned forward I could kiss her.

What did I mean? I didn't understand it, just that the moment she bound herself to me, I hadn't felt this whole in centuries. To tell her might scare her. I didn't want to risk it.

With her so close and nowhere to hide. My eyes flitted from her blue eyes to her full mouth—to the dimple hiding in her cheek when she smiled. It saddened me when she didn't smile; I liked that dimple. I leaned forward, close enough to feel her breath caress my face. My heart rate sped. I stopped breathing. Then the car stopped, and it felt like a bucket of ice cold water splashed my face. I exhaled a frustrated breath and reached for the door handle.

"Wait!" Julia grabbed my hand, pulling me back into the car. "Tell me," she begged. Her face inches away. I felt her heat against the side of my body.

"I enjoy having you around, babe." I leaned forward and kissed her chastely. She stared wide eyed. "Anyway, let's see if your boyfriend is at Bill's house."

"He's not my boyfriend anymore," she growled.

I giggled like a schoolboy.

We traversed up the pathway, my tail still wrapped around her ankle. Ossie ensured the coast was clear and morphed into his fighting demon. I followed suit and became my purple devil.

Julia glimpsed at me, and her cheeks reddened. I gave her a show of my goods and she laughed, shaking her head.

Ossie didn't bother knocking on the door. He blasted the door from its hinges and entered the dark house like the scary monster he was. It was exactly as we had left it, with one difference; the smell of the dead wafted in the air.

"I guess that's Bill's corpse we're smelling," Julia said as she headed for the stairs.

"But that's wrong, Bill should've turned into ash," Ossie said, passing Julia on the stairs, jumping four steps at a time and raced down the hallway.

We followed him into Bill's room. Bailey switched on the light. My eyes stung; taking a moment to get used to the brightness. Then I saw Bill's corpse.

Ossie ripped off the bedding, feathers floating around us.

Julia gasped and turned away.

Bailey paled and followed Julia out of the room.

Ossie and I stared at Desmond's body—shredded to pieces. His corpse a gruesome find; arms and legs sliced from his body, his eyes destroyed, tongue hanging out of his severed jaw and on the pillow. His destroyed organs covered the mattress. The flies, rot, and stench. Ick.

"He switched portraits," Ossie mumbled, but I heard what he'd said and I nodded.

I understood the moment I saw Desmond instead of Bill.

Julia cried behind me, muttering to herself. Her voice becoming louder as she approached. I turned to push her away—she'd seen enough.

"That's what I saw before. That's what enraged Bill before…," — she spluttered, — "before all this."

"I don't understand? What did you see?" I asked, placing my hands on her shoulders to keep her away from the grisly sight in the bed.

"Bill has an artist who paints replicas of famous paintings, then sells them to unsuspecting buyers. He probably did the same thing with his, but over one of Desmond. Then Seth thinks it's Bill when it's actually Desmond."

Slow clapping sounded behind us. I turned towards him.

Julia spun around and stood slightly behind me.

Bailey moved behind the chest of drawers and I felt heat from Ossie to my side.

"So clever, darling. I knew you saw *something*. To think you'd never tell. Tsk, tsk, tsk." Bill said, closing the gap. "And how is our *master*?" He taunted. His eyes flitting from mine then to Ossie's.

Ossie shook his head. "You can't get away with this."

"Really? Do you see our master here? No!" He yelled. "He's such an evil bastard who gets his little devils to do his work for him. Not anymore. He thinks I'm dead. When I'm done with you there's no-one to tell him what really happened."

Bill lunged at Ossie, slamming his claws into his chest. Ossie spun around in time and elbowed Bill on his back, sending him to the floor.

I let go of Julia and jumped onto Bill. Ossie joined me and yanked Bill's arm while I pulled the other. Bill screamed. We pulled as one, removing both arms at the shoulders.

Smoke wafted in the air. Bill's screams pierced our ears. Heavy booted footsteps sounded as men ascended the stairs, heading towards us.

Ossie slammed his clawed hand into Bill's chest.

A vampire screamed as she flew into the bedroom. I blocked her by shoving my sharp claws into her chest while Ossie destroyed our naughty vampire.

Her cries stopped when I yanked on the juicy black organ in my hand and pulled my arm out of her abdomen. She burst into angry flames, then a cloud of ash before floating away.

Cries sounded behind me; Julia and Bailey. Most likely

grossed out by our violent behavior. But I couldn't help them now; vampires were heading our way.

Another vampire jumped onto my back. His hands reached for my throat as my tail whipped his face, leaving a large gash in his cheek. I hit his jaw, and he stumbled away.

Glancing over my shoulder, Ossie pulled his scythe out from behind his back and held it above his head. He hated that weapon, but it's what he was. He sliced through Bill's neck removing his head. When Bill's body fell to the ground, Ossie dug into Bill's chest and removed his heart. Bill burst into flames then ash. The three vampires who approached burst into a cloud of ashy-smoke and rained on the tiled floor before hurting us.

Ossie stood upright and sheathed his scythe.

Bailey and Julia cowered in the corner.

"It's okay," I said, but knew we'd just scared the crap out of the girls. "Let's get out of here."

Chapter Twenty-Three

JULIA

No matter what I did, I couldn't get the vision of Desmond out of my mind; and then the vicious attack on Bill and his demise. Everything was too much. It was my first time exposed to such violence.

"Are you okay?" Os asked. His tone gentle and caring.

"No," I snapped, confused, as a flurry of emotions hit me all at once. I didn't know if I was coming or going.

Bailey parked in her driveway. No one moved. We sat in silence. The car seemed to vibrate with Ossie and Os' power, suffocating me.

I yanked the car door open and stumbled out.

"Let me help you." Os was beside me in a flash, helping me stand. I pushed him away.

"Give her a sec," Bailey said. "She'll come around," she added as she climbed out and headed towards her front door. "Come, I want to check the incantation and break your bonds."

While they entered Bailey's house, I sat on a lawn chair kept in the backyard and tried to forget about what I'd seen.

I needed to expel the evil feeling stuck within after witnessing so much blood and gore. I shuddered as visions of flesh tearing and bones popping flashed before me.

I folded my legs beneath me and leaned back, closing my eyes. It was dark, the night creatures out; owls, crickets, something digging in the trash. My eyes shot open but saw nothing. Thank goodness. The last thing I wanted to see was a critter eating rotten food.

I closed my eyes again and exhaled a shaky breath. My heart rate evened out; it no longer wanted to burst out of my chest. The breeze cooled my warm, damp skin. The smell of cut grass and fast food wafting in the air; along with trash. I opened my eyes again. Bailey needed to move her trash cans farther away from the back door.

I cleared my throat. And thought of… nothing.

Now that we'd destroyed Desmond and Bill, I no longer needed to hide from them. I didn't know what to do next. I was an accountant; I could find work easily.

The sound of cups placed on the counter behind me echoed along with a spoon hitting the sides. Bailey was most likely making tea. The sound of their voices carried through the silent night, but I couldn't discern what they were saying.

Seth had given them the correct incantation to sever the bond between Os and me. It had to be done. I couldn't remain tied to him forever. I had my own life. He had his. We had to do this.

I stood and approached the back door. As I entered the kitchen, they turned as one and smiled suspiciously—like they'd been talking about me. I ignored it.

"Let's get this done," I said. "I hope you made me a cup of tea."

"Of course." Bailey handed me a mug. "Before we start,

you need to understand there might be some pain. It was a blood incantation to bind yourself to Os and we'll need blood from both of you to break it. Ossie has given me the incantation from Seth and it looks good. So…" Bailey glanced from me to Ossie, then Os and back at me. "Are you ready?"

I stared guiltily at Os; pain reflected in his eyes.

"You want this? I mean, then you're free to do as you please," I asked him.

"Sure, I'll do it if you want it."

"I mean, of course, we want this. We need to get on with our lives. Don't we?"

Ossie and Bailey's heads kept moving from side to side as they watched the conversation between Os and me.

"Whatever you need, Julia. We can still live our lives and remain bound to one another; distance doesn't seem to hurt us. I'm just saying we have options." He shrugged nonchalantly. "Rather make an informed decision than regret it."

"How can I regret breaking the bond? You're an incubus and I'm human. We have our own lives. Anyway, I think it's for the best," I said, nodding. It was the right decision. I needed to move on. And so did Os. We were nothing to each other. We were barely friends. This had all been a mistake.

I might not read minds, but I saw pain in Os' eyes. I doubted he would miss me. How could he? We were bound for less than a week. He would thank me for his freedom. We needed to separate.

"Come, let's get this over with," I mumbled, and headed towards the living room.

The entire process took less than ten minutes to complete. Bailey placed a large salt circle around us, sliced our palms, and said the words.

The secured rope I'd felt attached to my chest dissolved, and I felt lighter... but emptier. No longer bound to Os, my chest no longer tight and the warm comfort disappeared—leaving me hollow. I shivered at the loss. Tears welled in my eyes and the back of my throat ached.

Os stared at me the entire time; from his expression, I could tell he didn't want this. He wanted to stay bound to me, but I couldn't understand why. I was just a human; a nobody. He could have anyone he wanted. I averted my eyes, but felt his gaze weigh down on me.

When Bailey finished, and stepped out of the circle. Os didn't move, and neither did I. When Bailey and Ossie left the room, I glanced up at Os. His glacier-blue-colored eyes held unshed tears, his mouth in a tight line and his hands balled into fists.

"I didn't want this you know," he finally said and approached. "I enjoyed having you around like a parasitic twin."

I burst out laughing while he smiled sadly.

"I know I'm a demon, an incubus, and you probably feel intimidated by it all... but... I was wondering if you'd give me a chance. Get to know all of me." He reached for my shoulders. I braced for the cold emptiness that would accompany it. Now that we were no longer bound, I'd feel nothing for him. But perhaps that's what I needed in order to let go. If I felt nothing, then I'd know we did the right thing separating.

And then he touched me.

His hands burned my flesh. His desire flared across my collarbone, up my neck, and down my spine. I shivered as all the hairs on my body stood up.

"And that's us, little mouse. I'm not using any of my special incubus powers on you. What's happening now is us.

And I'm afraid I can't let you go. Not when I've finally found you."

Os didn't give me a chance to respond. He closed the gap, cupped my face, and pressed his lips against mine. I melded into him. My hands roamed his chest. He stepped closer. I felt his muscles move beneath my palms as I wrapped my arms around him, pressing my hands into his back; I wanted him as close as possible. Heat from his body engulfed mine. I wanted to get lost with him.

Os' right hand gripped my head to keep me in place while his other caressed down the side of my neck, shoulder, waist, then back up.

His kiss was deep and thorough, bruising my lips and I wanted more.

I breathed him in; light aftershave, earth, and pepper.

Os moaned and pulled away. "I want more," he growled. "I want you," he said softly, gently, and with enough emotion to make me cry. He meant those words; he really did want me.

I yelped when he reached for my ass and lifted me. I clutched his neck, wrapped my legs around his waist and he walked us to my bedroom.

"You want to stay here or go to my room?" he asked when he kicked the door closed.

"Here's fine. I'm not ready to go to your place just yet." I smirked.

Os set me down on the bed, but still held me.

I giggled when he growled as he palmed my breast. "I love natural breasts, a handful is just perfect." He bit through my clothing, sending a sharp sensual pain straight to my core, then did the same to my other breast, and growled. "I want more. Get this off," he said, trying to tear my clothing off me.

"Hold your horses," I said, lifting my top off and unclasped my bra. But before I could do anything, Os removed my bra, grabbed my hands and placed both wrists in one of his enormous hands. Then he kissed his way down.

I sucked in a deep breath when he sucked on a nipple, pinching it between his teeth. The strange combination of his warm breath, the cold air and him holding me down left me needing more. I ground myself against him, making him grunt in pleasure.

"So needy, little mouse," he teased. Os glanced up, his light blue gaze taking me in, watching me as he worked his way down.

He unbuttoned my jeans with his free hand and pulled down. I lifted my butt off the mattress so he could remove my underwear and jeans at once, and without letting go of my hands.

I lay naked. Vulnerable and at his mercy. But he wasn't Desmond. Os would never do what Desmond did; how he forced my submission every single time. No. Osmodeus wasn't like that. Os wanted to please me; I could tell by the kindness in his eyes, and the gentle strength with which he held me.

"So beautiful," he hissed, letting my hands go and moved down, pushed my legs farther apart and settled himself right there and kissed me like he kissed my mouth.

My hands dug into the mattress as he sucked, licked, and teased my folds. The sensations like molten lava coursing through my veins. I bucked when my orgasm struck, sending waves of pleasure, one after the other.

Os didn't stop his sensual rhythm. Then, when he inserted two fingers and found that wonderful spot while his tongue continued its pleasurable wrath on that little button, a burst of colors clouded my vision as another orgasm struck.

It was an out-of-body experience. My skin tingled, my cheeks heated, and my body trembled.

Os hovered above me, kissed me so I could taste myself, and hummed. "You taste divine, little mouse."

I giggled. "Julia, my name is Julia," I said, opening my eyes.

"You're my little mouse, Julia." He kissed me chastely and pushed the head of his steel member against my sensitive folds. "Now are you ready for me, little mouse?" he asked, raising both eyebrows.

"Uh-huh," I said, "I am."

"Good, hold on tight," he said and the moment I clutched his shoulders, he entered my heated sheath.

I felt every inch of him as he slid in and out, finding his rhythm. With each measured stroke, I felt tension ease away. My body hummed with his pleasure as he loved my body with his and watched me intently.

It was not only pent up passion he released but also a part of him. I felt his raw emotions as if they were my own and they were real. He no longer hid behind his human form, or behind his jokes. This was the real Os.

When my eyes met his, they communicated his desire; the pain and desperation of not having found someone to call his own. Yes, he fed on many women, but never like this. He never loved their bodies with his. It was never this intense connection we shared as we formed our own bond.

It was in that moment that I'd consider being his and his alone, whatever that meant I didn't know, but I'd like to try.

His movements became uncoordinated as he neared his release. I held on tighter, wrapping my legs around his body, and met his thrust with my own.

My moan triggered his response, and he pounded into me without restraint. The feel of his body grinding against mine electric and I sang for him as our orgasms caught us at the same time.

Os held onto me as he stilled while I continued grinding into him to make my orgasms last longer. Then we fell into a comfortable silence as our heated bodies joined and we collected our breaths.

Chapter Twenty-Four

OS

I showered with Julia and couldn't keep my hands off of her. With each touch burning my palm and sending pleasurable heat through my chest, I knew I'd found the girl for me. Yes, she was human. Yes, she was fragile. But I could turn her into a succubus and she'd always be mine. Forever. Only time would tell whether she wanted the same thing. But for now, I'd enjoy every minute with my one and only.

Once clean and naked under the covers, we couldn't sleep and got up. We found Ossie and Bailey in the kitchen eating breakfast. The sun had risen, splashing golden rays across the couches and living room floor. The scene was surreal and heavenly.

"Well, well, well," Ossie chimed. "Look what the cat dragged in. So how did it go love birds?"

"Shut up, and none of your business." I brushed past my brother, ignoring his childish question.

"You look better," Bailey said, hugging Julia.

"I feel," — Julia glanced my way, — "refreshed." Her cheeks heated and accepted the mug of coffee I proffered.

Demons didn't need to eat or drink human food, but sometimes we indulged. Normally we fed on other things, but today I acted like a human and drank some coffee with my girl. Even Ossie was enjoying a cup. I stood beside Julia, draped my arm around her shoulders, and brought her closer. She held onto me and nestled under my arm.

Bailey stared at us with a knowing grin.

"What?" Julia asked.

"Well… I was wondering. Now that you two are… closer, should I bind you again?"

Julia glanced up at me and shrugged.

"I'd love to be, if Julia would have me. But it's her choice. And whatever it is, I'll still be here," I said, meaning every word.

"I don't know," Julia started. "If we joined again, I don't know how it would work. I mean, he's a demon. No offense," she said to me.

"None taken." I kissed her temple.

"I want to get to know you first; what it means to date a demon and understand what's expected of me."

"I expect nothing from you, little mouse. Let's date first and see how it goes. For now, stay here and I'll visit you. Then, I say this loosely because you don't have to, I'll change you."

"Then I'd become a succubus?"

"Yes, and you'll never age."

"But then I'd feed on men."

"No, if we're both demons, we feed on each other without draining ourselves. If we want more power, only then do we feed on others."

"Seriously?"

"As a corpse," I said.

She swatted my chest. "You and your corpses." She

laughed. "Maybe. Let's date and see where it goes. Who knows, I might not even like you." The lines near her eyes crinkled when she grinned.

"See, nobody had to decide on anything. Just a couple of consenting adults doing what makes us happy."

Julia squeezed my waist and didn't let go. It felt nice.

Chapter Twenty-Five

JULIA

I moved the centerpiece to the left, to the right, then gave up. I eventually left it in its original spot. I stood back and glanced at the table—everything was perfect, or as perfect as it could ever be.

Knocking sounded on my front door. My smile stretched my face in two and I approached the door, my hand hovering near the door handle. I opened the door and my smile dropped along with my heart.

"Please sign here," the delivery guy said, holding up a pen and clipboard.

I signed the document and handed him the items back. He gave me a large package. I kicked the door closed and placed the package on my kitchen counter.

As much as I didn't want to admit it, the package concerned me. One look at the clock and I knew Os was late. He was never late; in the six months we'd been dating, he had never been late before. But today he was half an hour late and instead of him standing on the other side of my front door, I received a package.

I grabbed the scissors and cut the string binding the package, then I ripped the brown paper off the box. I gasped. Once the package was open and the contents sitting on the counter, hot tears streamed down my cheeks.

Somehow, somewhere, Os had found the photo albums of my parents I'd thought lost after they had died. I only had one photo album with only a few pictures of them, but this... three photo albums filled with pictures of my parents. Including pictures of me growing up.

"Happy six-month anniversary," Os said behind me. My busy mind relaxed at the sound of his voice. His powerful hands gripped my shoulders, and I felt his heat beat against my back. I leaned into him; a calmness washing over me at his touch.

"How...?" I choked on the rest of my words and turned in his embrace.

"I have my ways," he said, kissing the tip of my nose. "Now where's my dinner, woman?" His tone playful yet demanding.

"You're late." I slapped his chest and hurried into the kitchen and removed the plates filled with food. "Sit, I'll bring it to you." Os didn't need to eat food, but he always indulged me so that I didn't have to eat alone.

Os sat at the head of the table and I beside him, presenting him with his plate of food. He poured champagne into our glasses and enjoyed a long sip.

Os told me about his day in the library with his brother. Since meeting them and our adventures together, the brothers realized they enjoyed working together and Os joined Ossie. Os preserved some of the much older tomes, while Ossie ensured nobody removed a book from his library.

Os presented me with another gift; placing it on the table in front of me after we'd eaten.

"Are you nuts?" I said, pushing it away. "Your brother will have your head for what you've done."

"I don't care." His grin was contagious, and I couldn't help but smile at him.

"I love it." I picked up the tome carefully, my fingertips caressing the handwritten title and author; *Mother Nature*. It's her diary.

"You have an hour and then I must take it back. Ossie has stepped out and should be back soon." He kissed my forehead. "I have a game to watch. When it's over, I must go." His expression turned serious, and I nodded.

While Os settled into his baseball game, I read Mother Nature's diary. I thought it lost, but Os had told me they kept it in one of their secret enclosures with many other important documents.

I carefully opened the cover and read the first page…

———

An hour later my eyes hurt, dust covered my fingers, and my mind buzzed with information.

"What? How…? Why…?" I shook my head. "Her children." I glanced at Os; his solemn expression struck my chest, and I ached for him. "*Your* mother." I swallowed hard. "When did you find out?"

Os closed the distance. His hand reached for me and his fingers curled around my neck possessively.

"When you mentioned you wanted to read her diary and asked whether it was at the library, I found it in a secret compartment. I read it and showed Ossie. He didn't want to believe it, but it all made sense. The more I thought about it, the more I didn't want to show you. Then you'd know who her children are—"

"You and Ossie."

He nodded. "And Maddox, Seth's son."

I nodded, letting the information sink in. "But it doesn't say who your father is." Os shook his head; he remained secretive with that information and I knew it spelled disaster if I found out. But I suspected it may be Victor but I would never say it out loud. Mother Nature enjoyed both brother's company and it might start a war if either knew about the other. "What does it mean? I won't say anything, obviously."

"I know, but if Seth finds out her diary is real, he'll tear down everything in his path until he has it in his hands. He is spiteful. He already hates Maddox for relinquishing his duties, Blaire transposing his powers to his younger brother; the lessor devil. And Mother Nature, who is still hiding." Os shook his head. "Who knows what Seth would do. So," — Os took the diary from me and tucked it in his coat, — "I need to take this back now."

"Will I see you later?"

"Of course." His grin reached his eyes. Then air popped in my face like a balloon and he left dust in his wake.

"Bye…" I said as an afterthought.

I cleaned the kitchen counter, washed the dishes, and enjoyed a long shower. While my body was busy, my mind kept thinking about Mother Nature's diary, and my first encounter with Os and these six months.

Then I remembered our first sexual experience and how our lives blurred together since then. I already felt like we had merged, forming one being where I'd know how he felt or he knew what I'd say next. We were a super cheesy couple, but I loved it.

Os had mentioned turning me into his succubus so that we could be together forever. But... Forever... An eternity with the same person. I wondered whether I'd become bored, or if he would. The risks were there, but with a greater reward. I knew in my heart he'd take care of me as I would him.

When my ex had tried to kill me, never in a million years would I think my next relationship would begin so soon after. I knew I didn't want to rush into the next relationship because the next person I'd love would be my last; I wanted him to learn everything about me—to want me warts, scars and all—to need me as much as I needed him, and to love me in slow motion.

I was such a hopeless romantic, considering everything I'd been through, but I loved Os with my heart and my mind—the largest sexual organ, and it was true for me. Os had bulldozed his way into my life and for six months he hadn't given up on me, hadn't made me cry, or made me think he had other intentions. He loved me for who I was; my scars, my wrinkles, and my baggage.

Os committed himself to this relationship. And I wanted him. The last piece to our puzzle was joining in holy matrimony, so that I could enjoy parts of his world I'd been too afraid to consider.

Chapter Twenty-Six

OS

I arrived at Julia's house surrounded by darkness. Usually she left her bedside lamp on after she'd gone to bed, but tonight darkness bathed her bedroom. Wind blew through the open window, making the curtain dance in the moonlight. A weight filled my stomach and bile rose, forcing me to swallow hard.

She'd been asleep in bed. Parts of her sheets lay crumpled on the floor from what I assumed someone had pulled the covers off her and dragged her away.

Regret filled my veins; I didn't kiss her goodbye or hold her in my arms one last time. Instead, I grabbed the diary from her and hurried to return it to the library before my brother returned.

Usually my emotions were in check. Until now. The woman I loved more than anything in the world was missing. Gone. Taken. But who? We weren't at war with anyone. The Underworld was at rest.

But that didn't mean—

The bathroom door opened behind me, interrupting my thoughts. Julia exited the dark bathroom, yawning and with one hand in her disheveled hair. She glanced up at me and her face lit up.

"You used the bathroom with the light off?"

"Yeah, I wasn't sure what time you'd get in and didn't want to wake up." She wrapped her arms around my middle, hugging me. "But now that you're here." I felt her warm breath through my shirt, followed by her kiss.

I pulled Julia closer, and I never wanted to let go. I never wanted to feel that moment of panic or experience fear coursing through my veins again.

"What's wrong?" she asked, her cheek still against my chest. When I didn't answer, she pushed away from me and flicked on the light switch. "What's going on? Did your brother beat you up or something?"

I wrestled with myself and whether to tell her how vulnerable I felt when I thought someone had taken her. And I didn't want her to think less of me. I was the strong one, her protector, not the other way around.

"Hey, what's going on behind those eyes? Tell me," Julia whispered, her tone gentle as she cupped one side of my face, forcing me to look her in the eyes.

I couldn't keep my thoughts to myself. I had to tell her. "For a moment, I thought someone had kidnapped you." My eyes flitted to the sheets on the floor and the open window. The moonlight casting its silver tendrils across the floor and bed. "That you always leave a light on for me."

"Oh, babe, I'm so sorry." She rocked onto her toes and kissed me. Her lips warm and tender while she filled her kiss with so much love I felt it touch my soul.

I pulled her closer, needing to feel all of her.

"Babe? You're squashing me," she said through our kiss.

I relaxed my arms, and she sucked in air.

"Sorry, did I hurt you?"

"No," she said, but the lines between her eyes were still visible. "And why would anyone come for us?" She shrugged, grabbing me by the hand and dragging me to bed. "And besides, everything is fine." Her smile reached her eyes.

"What do you want to do?" I wiggled my eyebrows.

"I'm ready, Os," she said seductively.

"For what?"

She frowned harder. "You're an idiot sometimes, you know that. What do you think?"

Only one thought came to mind. "To be my mate?" Hope fluttered inside my chest and my skin warmed at the thought.

She nodded. Her eyes glistened in the dim light.

I kissed her chastely. "Are you sure? It's forever."

"Yes, make me yours. Now!"

She didn't have to tell me twice. I ripped my clothing from my body, then removed hers as delicately as my claws would allow. Just thinking about having her as my mate for all eternity caused my inner demon to roar in ecstasy.

"Do you remember what I told you?" I asked. She nodded. "You know not to be afraid?" She nodded again, her smile widening. "I will never hurt you. You are mine. My true mate. And I'd rather die than hurt a hair on your pretty little head."

"Okay, I get it," she said, slapping my arm.

"You ready?"

"Uh-huh."

I kissed her one last time and arched my back. My clawed hands dug into the mattress and I was sure I tore her duvet, but I didn't want to tear my eyes away from her. I needed to ensure she continued feeling safe around me.

My purple tail swished behind me. My skin shimmered as my true form changed the handsome man Julia lusted over, leaving behind an incubus. A demon. Me.

I didn't need a mirror to know my victims could drown in my black eyes; but Julia was far from a victim, or that my teeth extended and sharper; one bite and my victims would suffer the poison I released and bleed to death. But I wouldn't bite her.

I flicked out my forked tongue, tasting her scent—heaven. My hair disappeared and my horns extended out of my forehead.

My skin not only changed color but hardened—a protection mechanism against most weapons; man made or supernatural.

I moved between her legs, my cock rock hard and needing to enter her delicious soft and moist flower.

Julia opened her legs wider, allowing me all the access I wanted.

I grunted in pleasure. She whimpered in anticipation. I lowered myself with a hand on either side of her head. Her pupils dilated, mouth parted, her breath short and shallow.

"My little mouse. What will I do with you?" I taunted. "It's your last chance, Julia," — I lowered my body, so she only felt my heat and not my rough skin. I wanted her to crave me as I craved her, — "because once I start, there's no turning back," I said near her ear. My voice deep and throaty. I watched her shiver. She blinked and nodded. "Not good enough, little mouse. You need to say the words—"

"I want you Os. Take me. I'm yours. Turn me. Forever."

That was my cue to do as she pleaded. I pushed the head of my throbbing cock inside her, devastatingly slowly.

Julia moaned as I filled her, inch by inch, until I was balls deep inside.

I shivered as she clenched around me, her heat engulfing me. Oh, my gods, this was delicious. This was the first time making love to her in my demon form; the only way to turn her into my mate; to change her into my demon queen.

I would cherish this moment of her giving up control and handing it to me as I claimed not only her body, but her soul. And her heart I would care for as if my own. She was mine; I was hers.

I thrusted into her, hard and fast, then slowed my rhythm. Julia moaned in frustration and I picked up speed again. She held onto me, our skin damp and touching; she didn't seem to mind my rough exterior.

My demon power oozed out of my pores and latched onto her, seeping into her skin. Julia tightened her grip on my arms, her nails digging into my hard flesh. She wrapped her legs around my body and her muscles clenched around my cock once more.

I continued thrusting as my power became one with her. When her orgasm struck, her eyes flitted open. When she focused on me, black eyes stared back in wonder. My power was succeeding.

I pounded into her, tearing moans from her, and I almost stopped when I saw blood on her lips. But in time, she would get used to her sharp teeth.

With each powerful thrust, more of my power claimed Julia.

With the build-up of another orgasm threatening to rip her apart, I slammed into her harder, faster, and gripped her tighter.

Julia's orgasm ripped through her. My orgasm struck

like lightning. The ground shuddered beneath us and something whipped my ass. I glanced over my shoulder and saw a second tail swooshing with mine.

I beamed down at Julia, my purple succubus, and warmth filled my heart.

"That was," — Julia swallowed and cleared her throat, — "strange, exciting, powerful, and I want more."

"Easy little mouse. First get used to what you have." I eased out of her, immediately feeling the loss of her.

"No, stay, don't go," she whined.

I stared at her for what felt like hours and, wearing a stupid smile, she finally spoke. "You're acting weird. What do I look like?"

"Beautiful."

"Ah, but seriously. How bad is it?"

"You're a much prettier version of me."

Her laugh filled the room. She sat up and slowly climbed off the bed. She leaned one hand against the wall for balance and carefully walked towards the mirror. When she saw herself, her silence filled me with dread. I flew off the bed and stood by her side.

"It's okay, honey. You're still beautiful. And remember, you can change your appearance. You can look like the old you. With me by your side to help you practice, you can do so much—"

Julia placed one purple talon on my lips, cutting my sentence.

"I'm not upset. I'm in awe, Os. It's, I don't know, weird, but I love it. I really do. And look," — she swished her tail again and smacked my ass, — "now we can have tail fights."

"I'd advise against it. Ossie and I used to do it when we were kids and it hurts. We'll bleed. So no," — I shook my head, — "no tail fights. But we can tickle fight." I grabbed her and tickled all her favorite spots.

"No, stop it," she screamed and disappeared. She reappeared on the bed and laughed. "How did I do that?"

"Come here, little mouse," — I proffered a hand, — "allow your man to show you the way."

Chapter Twenty-Seven

JULIA

The silver moon tendrils crept along the bedroom floor, illuminating the dark bed. The man, Mark—my first victim —slept peacefully.

I crept towards Mark. His breath hitched. I froze. He turned onto his back, his right hand on his chest with his left hand near his thigh.

I closed the distance. Carefully, I climbed onto Mark's bed, straddling his upper thighs. The moment I touched him, he moaned as if in a nightmare. I hesitated.

"Don't stop," Os breathed beside me. "You'll love it. And so will he."

"I feel bad, like I'm taking advantage of him." We'd gone over this so many times. I felt like a rapist; a dirty, disgusting bad person. I didn't want to do this, but Os suggested I try it once.

"We feed on their sexual energy, my love. We do not rape. We do not touch them indecently. We merely bring out of them what they desire. And it's that which sates our hunger."

I knew Os was right, but I still felt terrible; my human side still quite dominant compared to my horny demon side.

I exhaled a shaky breath and leaned forward, a hand on either side of Mark's shoulders. He remained asleep. I leaned closer and blew gently on his exposed chest and I watched as all the fine hairs stood up.

He shivered but didn't turn onto his side.

I moved forward a bit and gently blew on his cheek. He moaned pleasurably and shifted slightly so that his pelvic area was near mine.

I blew again on his other cheek and elicited the same response, except this time I felt his erection press against me. Heat blossomed between my legs. My body warmed from the inside out, and an overwhelming need engulfed me.

My tail swished behind me. My talons grew, and I felt my teeth elongate. I wanted to ravage Mark, but not only enjoy his erotic essence, but literally eat him. I wanted to drink his blood, taste his flesh and swallow every morsel; visions of him chewed open while I devoured every inch of him should send me running for the hills. Instead, it consumed me with a frenzy I hadn't experienced before.

I whipped my head to the side so Os could see my dilemma. He grinned. I frowned harder.

"Hectic isn't it."

"Why didn't you warn me?"

"What? And miss out on all the fun."

I placed one foot on the floor to climb off Mark, but Os reached for me, keeping me in position.

"Stay, control your hunger, and it will be over in a moment." He removed his hand and winked. "Trust me."

"I hope so, because right now I want to dig into his soft belly."

Os chuckled behind me. I glared daggers at him. He pointed at the man who moved beneath me.

I returned my leg to its original position and raised my body off Mark and waited until he was comfortable before sitting again; on his thighs. I didn't feel like having his hard cock pressed against my tender flesh. Every time that happened, I thought of blood, organs, and chewing on his bones.

I shuddered in disgust.

Exhaling again, I blew against his chest.

"Now breathe in his essence, my little mouse."

Nodding, I did as Os suggested and closed my eyes while I breathed in. The ravenous feeling of tearing into the man's body evaporated and in its place was tranquility; an oasis in the desert, a waterfall after a long, hot hike. My salvation.

A calmness brushed against my chest, easing my fear of hurting Mark. He was enjoying himself while I fed on one yummy 'bite' at a time.

I opened my eyes and watched the man enjoy a sexual dream. His cock hard and needing release. The man reached for his steel member and stroked himself.

My juices flowed, and I desperately wanted to sit on him and ride him into next week.

But I didn't touch him. Watching him masturbate in his sleep was the equivalent of finding a pot of gold. Instead, I absorbed his sexual energy one breath at a time until I felt lightheaded.

When hands grabbed my shoulders and helped me off the bed, I came back to earth and leaned against Os.

"You were about to collapse, my little love-drunk mouse." Os kissed the top of my head. "Come, let's enjoy each other's bodies at home."

"I'd like that very much," I mumbled. My lips felt thick, my mind foggy, but all I wanted was Os.

My first time enjoying sexual energy was like downing shots all night while doing the Macarena and I was sure I'd have a hangover tomorrow morning.

It was fun even though I had my doubts at first. But I knew in my heart I didn't hurt Mark. I only enjoyed something natural in the air for me to absorb.

And right now, all I wanted was to ravage Os's body.

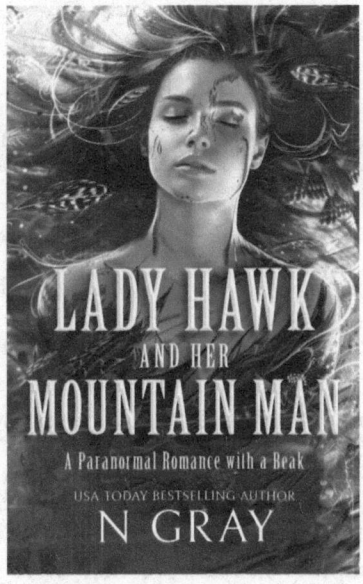

Lady Hawk and her Mountain Man: Chapter One

JANE

I watched from my perch. My enclosure large enough in case I shifted into my human form. But since my capture six weeks ago, I hadn't changed. Not for them. Ever.

It was dangerous staying in my animal form, but it was a risk I was willing to take. I'd rather face those risks than face the dangers that lie ahead.

With my captors fast asleep, they were awaiting their next orders or for morning, whichever came first.

A mouse scurried across the floor, found crumbs dropped when my captors ate, and disappeared into a hole in the wall.

My mouth salivated. It had been too long since I'd eaten—not by choice. The mouse looked tasty. I wanted to nibble on its soft meat. Better yet, I'd love to bite into my captors' soft bellies. They had more meat around their middle and I'd be killing two captors with one satisfactory stone.

Captor One snored, his enormous belly rising and falling as he dreamed of something. He was the strongest of the two, big and burley. He was all muscle, hardly any brain. Well, that's what I thought, anyway.

Captor Two was a skinny man with enough meat to keep me full for a few days. He was the weakest of the two, but a great archer. He hit his target every single time. Ever since I'd been here, I watched him practice on the target across the room, and he never missed. If he ever aimed at me, his arrow would strike. And I didn't need him to threaten me either, because I knew he would aim true.

The lights flickered on, momentarily blinding me. I screeched. The room painfully bright, I cowered in my darkest corner.

The captors awoke with a jolt.

Captor Two raised his bow and pointed his arrow at me. Even in a dreamy state, his reflexes were sharp and trained on me.

Their leader, Rhett, entered the room. He held his head up high, combed his fingers through his dark hair, and his black eyes shimmered with knowledge. I didn't like this look. He was cruel, and I imagined what he'd do next. Whatever he planned never ended well for me.

Trailing behind Rhett was my Michael—my protector. His body bruised and broken. His torn clothing caked with blood. Blood he'd spilled for me. Blood he'd gladly give to protect me. It broke my heart watching him suffer. I wanted to give in to Rhett's demands, but Michael had said, 'no'. I needed to stay in my hawk form and never give in to Rhett's demands, no matter what he did to Michael.

"Jane, I'm glad to see you're still awake. It would be much simpler if you just changed," Rhett groaned, emphasizing the word 'changed'. He reached for the clothing I'd first worn, bringing it towards his nose, and breathed deeply.

I shuddered and squawked, flapped my wings as I

showed my disapproval. Some of my feathers floated around me like snow flurries.

The evening was cool and I suspected winter was near. I needed all my feathers to stay warm.

"Change for me Jane. If you care about Michael. Do it!" Rhett growled, his glassy black eyes boring holes into me. I shivered at the thought. I knew what he was capable of. As hard as it was for me not to give in, I couldn't or Michael's torture would be for nothing.

Rhett harrumphed. "Michael doesn't have much longer, my dear. Do you want him dead?" Rhett raised his hand, pointed two fingers at Michael, and slashed his fingers in the air like knives. Two slashes formed on Michael's broad naked chest, followed by blood.

I squawked again.

"Don't do it, Jane," Michael mumbled. His lips swollen and cracked. The skin around his eyes finally healing and could see me. His blue eyes filled with sadness and with little strength he had left. I didn't know how much longer he had to live, but he was suffering. Every day since our capture, Rhett had tortured him. Slowly, Michael was dying because of me.

Rhett approached the cage with long tweezers, reached inside, and removed one of my golden feathers. My feathers no longer as golden, but a faded yellow. He placed the feather into a contraption to measure the gold content. It flashed red.

Rhett shook his head. "You're weakening, Jane. If I can't get what I need for the elixir, you're messing with my entire production line. Do you understand the conse-quences?" he said gravely.

I kept quiet, staring at him with my beady black eyes through the bars.

"Your kind will die with you if you don't do what I ask. I'm here to help you—"

"No, you're not. All you want is her precious feathers," Michael spluttered, blood dripping out of his mouth while his chest wound continued pumping blood. They weren't helping him. They weren't seeing to his wounds. They were leaving him to die like a wild animal.

I turned my focus on Rhett and wanted to pick at his soft eyeballs. They would be a tasty treat I'd savor and remember for the rest of my life.

"That's where you're wrong, *protector*. I want to ensure her kind lives on. I will breed with her, create more little hawks and watch them flourish. And if their gold is as pure as their mothers, then we'll all be happy for it. It's a win-win situation," Rhett grinned. His dark eyes flashed with murky oil. He was evil to the core.

I didn't know what flavor evil Rhett was, I only sensed he was one of the worst. Rhett didn't shift into any creature, nor did he drink blood. But there was something about him I sensed was pure evil. It was possible he was the devil's spawn—created to unleash his wicked deeds.

"It's time to decide, Jane," Rhett continued, pacing in front of my cage. "Michael won't last much longer." Rhett raised the same hand, slicing his fingers through the air once more.

I screeched.

Michael collapsed to his knees, gripping his neck to stop the bleeding, but his life essence pulsed between his fingers; his carotid artery shredded.

"Don't give in to him, Jane," Michael said in a hoarse voice. "Don't. I signed up to protect you now and forever. Allow me to die with honor."

Rhett laughed as he left. "One more day, Jane," he sang as he disappeared out the room.

The two men who held Michael left him where he'd fallen and disappeared with Rhett.

My two captors did nothing but stare at Michael as he bled.

Michael crawled on weak limbs towards the cage. Ignoring his deep wounds, he still only cared for me, wanting to protect me.

My heart broke. More feathers fell. I flapped my wings, desperately needing to get out. I needed to save my Michael. He was dying because of me.

"Don't give in to him, Jane," Michael whispered, his face near the bars. "Get out of here. Once you're out, get your strength back. Understand that Rhett will never stop coming after you. You need to kill him. I know you can. Do it. Don't let this be in vain," Michael said weakly as he glanced at the captors, then turned back to me. "Grab my bracelet and fly away, Jane. Don't come back to save me. Nothing can save me now, but you can save yourself," Michael said softly, pulling a key from his back pocket and silently unlocked my cage.

Somehow he'd gotten the key—it was a risky move, but I appreciated it.

Slowly, Michael stood with the last of his energy; his legs shaky as more blood flowed down his body. As he yanked the door open, he lunged at my captors before they could react.

"Fly, Jane!" Michael yelled as a blade flashed in the air, striking Michael's chest.

I flapped my wings, was out of my cage, and grabbed the golden bracelet from the hook on the wall. When I'd secured the bracelet in my beak, I flew to the window. The window wide enough for me to squeeze through, and then I was out.

I couldn't turn back to see if Michael was okay. I knew he wouldn't be, not after seeing Captor One stab him. If I went back, it would be the end of me. They'd put me back inside my cage until I withered away.

I caught a wind pocket, flapped my large wings with all the energy I had left, and flew as hard and as fast as I could. But I was weak. My body was hurting, all the while mourning the loss of Michael. But I couldn't give up now. I had to do what Michael said; leave, get healthy, and find my way back.

Captor Two yelled out the window.

I didn't look behind; I needed to get far away quickly.

Something thwished, then whooshed past me. An arrow missed my right wing. Then the air changed as another arrow zipped past, closer this time.

All I focused on was getting away. I pushed my tortured body to fly harder and faster. I could never survive another round of torture, nor would I give Rhett the satisfaction.

Before I soared higher, another arrow thwished through the air, but this time it didn't go past. It struck my wing.

Lady Hawk and her
Mountain Men: Chapter Two

BYRON

The axe cut through the log with ease, splitting it into two manageable sizes for firewood. A motorized sound caught my attention. I dropped the axe, picked up my shirt, and wiped my brow. I spied my Glock near my water bottle and stepped closer in case I needed it.

In the distance I saw dust. Then the vehicle slowly came into focus. It was just Paul, the local grocery store owner. He pulled up in his large all-terrain vehicle and killed the engine. For a large, imposing man he was awfully friendly even with dark eyes, unbrushed brown hair and a bushy beard. He reminded me of a grizzly bear with a heart of gold, but just as deadly.

He grunted as he climbed off his ATV and approached. "Christ, the older I get, the harder it is getting off these things," he mumbled, dusting his jeans.

I chuckled lightheartedly, watching this burly man dismount from his ATV.

"I got your message," he said with one outstretched hand to shake mine.

"You didn't have to reply in person," I said with humor and slapped his back while we did that sideways manly hug.

"I'm on my way to the store, anyway," he said, surveying the area. Coming here was completely out of his way, but I appreciated the effort. He glanced from my head to my toes with a faint smile on his face. "I'm waiting for my delivery before I can deliver yours. I'll get one of my guys to bring your food parcel tomorrow, maybe throw in a candy bar. You're looking thin."

"I'm fine. You know how it is out here. Besides, the last thing I need is a trip to the dentist." Although I was running low on food, I was going hunting this afternoon, anyway. I'd just cut enough meat to last the week.

"Anyway, I guess I'll be off then," Paul said, stepping backwards. If I didn't know any better, I'd say he hesitated.

"I'll let you know if I need anything else." I moved with him. "Don't look so worried."

"You know I don't like you living out here on your own."

"I'm a big boy—"

"I know you can handle yourself," he said with an undercurrent of concern. "Anything can happen out here. And if you're alone, it's only that much harder."

"I'm fine, really. Thanks for checking in on me."

Paul checked up on me once a month, but this was his second time already. I slapped his back as he mounted his ATV and sat there, staring at me. Paul and I went way back and knew what each could handle. But him staring at me like that left me concerned, even though there was nothing for him to worry about.

"The wife wants you over for dinner next week. Can you make it?"

"I'll see what I can do."

Paul smiled, knowing I would make an excuse not to go. Their house was about a three-hour hike back towards town. I'd been there a few times since I'd moved here, but had declined the last couple of invites. They owned property that bordered on the outskirts of Sterling Meadow and the forest. They, like me, preferred nature to humans, but they still needed some human contact—I didn't.

I watched Paul leave. He didn't turn around like he always did. Then he disappeared.

I chopped the rest of the firewood and packed them near the cabin. Once the area was clean, I readied myself for the hunt.

———

It's dark. The only sounds came from insects; they kept me company with their stridulating music. They kept my mind focused and in the zone.

There's a slight breeze from the South. The temperature had dropped three degrees since I'd been out here. But nothing could stop me from getting my target.

Movement in the shadows caught my eye. I pointed my rifle in that direction and peered through the scope; a deer in my crosshairs.

My stomach rumbled. Paul was right. I hadn't eaten in two days and had to eat tonight. I'd placed my monthly order a little late this month and suffered the consequences. It was my fault. I used to have a standing order, which I changed since I didn't always get through some of the tinned food. I had rice left, but it wasn't the same as protein.

A chill swept through me. The cold, moist air could hamper my shot. But I'd used my rifle in worse temperatures before. I could make the shot easy.

I pressed my finger gently on the trigger, the connection automatic, almost sacred.

The deer moved from behind the tree and in the kill shot. I didn't hesitate. I exhaled and pulled the trigger, maintaining my position. The deer fell with a satisfactory thump.

My clothing stuck to my skin. My heart rate slowing as I kept watch through the scope for any other movement. There was none. No matter how many times I did it, I still felt the aftereffects; the adrenaline dump, then the shakes.

I pocketed the shell casing and picked up my weapon. The surrounding forest deadly quiet, not even the crickets were active. The deer lay where I'd dropped her; one shot to the head. She didn't suffer. She didn't know what hit her. It calmed me to know I hadn't hurt her. I only hunted to eat. I didn't kill on purpose anymore.

I placed my rifle on the ground, unsheathed my hunting knife, and only took what I needed. I said a prayer once I'd packed my meat into packaging and into my backpack. The wild cats, mountain lions, or even the wolves would eat the rest. I wasted nothing, as nature had intended.

The hike back to my cabin took longer. The wind had picked up and rain had fallen.

I preferred not to hunt where I slept—I didn't want any predator near my home apart from me. I didn't want to kill unnecessarily.

After they'd discharged me, I cashed in what money I had, bought a piece of land near water in the mountains, and built my home. A one bedroom cabin with everything I needed. It was enough for me to live comfortably and off the earth.

The tranquility of my home kept me here. I didn't mind going into the nearby town, Sterling Meadow. I just preferred to live away from others. I already had my fill of evil beings and the company they kept. And I'd destroyed enough lives to last me ten lifetimes. The less I saw of others, the better for my sanity. I chose to live out here with nobody around except me and nature.

My nights were quiet with no man-made sounds; cars, trucks, digging or other. It was only me, the quiet of nature, and the soothing animal and insect sounds.

By the time I reached my cabin, the weather had worsened, and it was dark. I went around back to start the generator. I switched on a light and dropped my backpack on the kitchen counter. The wind continued beating against the walls and roof—a cacophony of sounds echoing within the walls.

Before doing anything else I checked the laundry, bedroom and bathroom—all was as I had left it. The cabin smelled of gun oil, wood, and hints of coffee with my mug still on the kitchen counter from this morning.

Once content nobody had entered my place, I cleaned fat off the meat and chopped it into smaller portions. I bagged the steaks and placed them in the deep freeze.

I rounded my shoulders; pain laced down my right-hand side. My body aching from holding the same position for hours. A massage would be great, but only one thing helped.

Outside my cabin, I had a natural hot spring. That's one reason I chose this spot—for that hot spring. It comprised a whole heap of natural minerals which didn't hurt.

I exited my cabin and stripped naked. The chill of the wind caressed my skin. I brushed sand and dried blood from my ankles. I hadn't realized I'd hurt myself until I saw the gash above my ankle bone. Luckily, I didn't need stitches.

I climbed into the hot rocky pool; the contradicting

sensations from my chilled body in the hot spring knocked my breath away. But I instantly felt better and relaxed in the heated water.

The rock pool was small enough for three adults to sit comfortably. You couldn't dive in or you'd break your neck. But deep enough to stand in, reaching my chest.

Surrounding the pool were natural jets that filled the hot spring with scalding water, which cooled as it reached the surface.

I sunk below the surface to wet my face and hair. My feet touching the bottom rocks with grassy patches in between. The heat from the natural jets struck my aching muscles in my back, and I instantly relaxed against the rocky sides and glanced up at the sky. The tension building slowly seeping away as the wound on my ankle itched and I exhaled slowly.

After about twenty minutes, the weather threatened to blow me away. I climbed out, dried with a towel I'd kept outside, and already the wound on my ankle had healed— leaving behind a thin scab.

I wondered what was inside the water that gave it the healing properties, but I'd never question it. It was a blessing I'd gladly accept. It amazed me nobody had found it before I stumbled upon it.

One day I went hiking in search of land to call home and I literally fell into it. A thin layer of moss had covered the surface of the hot spring and I was so focussed on my surroundings I hadn't noticed the water until I fell into it. Then when I noticed my aching joints easing, I enquired about purchasing this land, and the government accepted my offer. Even after investigating the hot springs' origins, I'd found out nobody knew of its existence. I didn't tell Paul about it in case word got out, and he was my friend. I thought of it as something for me to protect. Should others find out about it, they may destroy it.

Once dressed I fried a steak and ate. Then I enjoyed a cup of tea on my porch. All the cabin lights were off. The pond and the forest beyond my front yard all bathed in moonlight. The pond water rippled with silver light was therapeutic to witness, with the stars bursting with their brilliance.

I sat peacefully in my chair, listening to the howling wind and watching the soft rain seep into the ground. The heaviness of the day fading as the chamomile tea and surroundings calmed me.

The sounds of a nearby hooting owl caught my attention. Stridulating crickets sounded behind my cabin. And leaves crunched underfoot as animals walked past. These were the sounds I wanted to hear.

The smell of rain filled the air as I breathed in through my nose, with dampness clinging to my jacket. I suspected a storm approaching from the north, and would feel the force of it by tomorrow.

My hackles raised the moment a stillness filled the space. I didn't hear what had caused it, but I sensed *something*. Not sure what it was, but I needed to investigate.

I placed my mug on the floor beside my chair and reached for the secret compartment at my feet, unsheathed a hunting knife, and grabbed my Glock with the silencer. I closed the lid on the compartment and stood up.

My porch had a few creaks, so instead of using the stairs I jumped over the railing onto soft ground, muffling my landing.

Somewhere behind my cabin I heard a sound; muffled cries of an animal.

Gentle rain sprinkled on my shoulders. The ground

damp with puddles. In a crouched position, I ran around my cabin, sticking to the shadows. My eyesight was good but I couldn't see far without my night goggles; I'd placed them in another compartment in the cabin, but out of reach. I would make do with what I had and continued in the sound's direction.

Another hunter, perhaps?

I'd encountered two hunters since living here. They were friendly. But I learned never to trust anyone. There could be a child with a doll in one hand and a grenade in the other. I trusted nobody.

Squinting up ahead, a shadow moved, stumbling. It was an injured animal or someone trying to ambush me.

I approached quietly, blending with the surrounding darkness.

Whimpering sounds came from that direction. Someone crying. The sounds were mournful and filled with pain.

I lowered my weapon but kept it ready with my knife firmly in my left hand—ready to slice and dice if I needed to.

The person tried to stand but kept falling, reminding me of a toddler trying to walk. I furrowed my brows as I neared. Not believing what I was seeing, I edged on closer without them noticing me.

If I didn't know any better, I'd assume it was a boy; short hair, slim body. But when I saw her naked breasts, I knew something was wrong. This was a trap. No woman stood naked in the middle of the forest. And to watch her unable to walk screamed suspicious—this was one trap I wouldn't fall for.

Why was she here?

She could be a witch needing body parts. A shifter

trying to change. A vampire needing blood. Or something else.

I needed to understand what she was and why she's here —and alone. I waited five minutes for others to join her but nobody did. It was only her battling to stand.

Her cries continued. Her left arm kept going to her right shoulder as she struggled to her feet. Something was wrong. Possibly injured.

I neared, taking a wider girth around her. I sensed nobody else. No footprints in the sand or disturbed bushes. There were no insects here either. And the only sounds came from her.

I approached from the back and cleared my throat.

"Hello? Is someone out there?" she said. Her voice meek and filled with pain. "I need help... hello?"

"What are you doing here?" I asked gravely as I showed myself, aiming my weapon at her head.

She raised her left arm, her right arm limp against her side with an arrow through her shoulder, and blood pouring down her side.

"What happened?" I pointed my weapon at her shoulder, then back at her head.

"Please, I'm hurt and mean you no harm. Can you help me get it out and then I'll be on my way," she cried. A soft whimper escaped her lips when she tried to stand.

"Are your legs injured?"

"No, I... um... please, I need help?"

I glanced around, but there was nobody else out here except us. There was no one about to jump out and kill me, us.

As much as I didn't want to take her inside my cabin, I couldn't leave her out here alone. But finding a naked, injured woman in the forest with nobody else around was irregular. She was trouble and could bring trouble to me.

But if anyone needed help, I was the right person. I could help her, even though I didn't want to. Although I didn't want trouble in my life, I couldn't leave her on her own when I knew I was capable of assisting.

"I don't want trouble," I said, echoing my thoughts.

"I don't mean to bring you any. But if you help me, I'll leave soon after. I promise. I don't want anyone else getting hurt because of me." She wiped her cheeks. She was crying.

Christ, I hated tears. I couldn't leave her out here, even though I didn't understand how she got hurt or how she got here. But she was naked, unarmed, and bleeding.

I sheathed my hunting knife inside my belt near my back and secured my weapon beside it. I needed to carry her, but she was very naked and I didn't know how best to pick her up without either of us feeling uncomfortable. She didn't seem too concerned with her nudity, but it bothered me. I hadn't seen another woman in over a year, never mind a naked one. I exhaled a shaky breath, removed my warm jacket, and handed it to her.

"Thank you," she said and slipped her left arm inside, then only covered her right shoulder in such a way that the protruding arrow didn't ruin my top, but still covered her flesh. She made an *ooh* sound and snuggled into my jacket. "This feels good. It's so, so warm." A smile tugged on her lips and for a moment I felt something... joy.

"Can you stand?" I asked. The uneasiness I'd felt earlier was back now that I actually had to touch her.

She shook her head. "No, I haven't... uh... in a while."

I didn't know what she meant. "I can't treat you out here so I'll need to pick you up." I motioned at her legs. "You're naked." I stated the obvious. "Are you okay if I, uh, touch you under your legs?" I didn't say I might need to touch her ass, but I'd get to that part if I needed to. I just hoped my erection didn't get bigger.

"Uh-huh," she mumbled, and got comfortable, ensuring my jacket remained closed over her breasts and other parts I could no longer see.

I swallowed hard as I stared down at her delicate form, and something tugged in me. Unsure of what that was, and ignored it. I needed to treat her wound and get her on her way again.

The rain continued drizzling, wetting her hair and porcelain skin. She licked her fine lips. My eyes darted to her long legs and feet.

I had to just get this over with, touch her bare legs and press her body against mine as I carried her. It was easy and I could do it. Christ, when visions of her naked body flashed before me again, I swallowed hard. A nervousness swept through me, reminding me of my teenage years.

This was stupid. I was being ridiculous.

Then, in one swift motion, I reached for her. My left arm slipped under her knees. My right hand snaked around her back and under her right arm without touching the arrow.

Christ, she could fit easily in my arms. And that strange tugging sensation happened again.

She was warm against my chest. Her skin soft against my fingertips, and she smelled of flowers; lavender, roses, and something else.

She wrapped a slender left arm around my neck, flinching as she moved her right hand to keep my jacket closed and without moving the arrow too much.

In one swift motion, I lifted her up, her side completely

against my chest and jeans. I hoped my belt buckle wasn't cutting into her flesh.

"Is this okay?" I asked. "Nothing cutting into you?"

"No, I'm fine." She smiled sweetly, although I sensed she was in a lot of pain.

"What's your name?" I asked, keeping the moment light and to get my mind off her naked body against mine. I hoped she couldn't feel my growing erection digging into my jeans.

"Jane," she said, looking me in the eye. The color of her irises was a mixture of grass green with hints of honey-brown. Her nose thin and dainty, her lips thin and parted, and her cheek-bones high. She would be beautiful if not for the emaciated appearance. Starved and bleeding; I didn't know if she would survive the night.

I glanced down at the slender slope of her neck and relieved my jacket covered most of her. But the top part of her breast showed, and I groaned inwardly. *Fuck!* She was beautiful and here I was, pawing her like a wild animal with my large hands.

I didn't know if she felt uncomfortable having a stranger carry her, but I sure felt uncomfortable carrying a half-naked, injured woman.

"I'm Byron," I said, introducing myself and traversed down the path towards my cabin.

I felt like the only person in the world when she smiled at me.

Jane was a lightweight, which added fuel to my suspicion that she was undernourished. With each step she flinched, but didn't cry out. It hurt me to feel her subtle movements without alerting me to the fact that she was in pain, but I saw it on her face. To ease her discomfort, I tried stepping lighter.

Finally, we reached my cabin, and I watched her expression change from hurt to wonder.

"Wow, your place is beautiful," she said. Her eyes glistening in the moonlight.

I traversed up the porch stairs, pulled the door handle down and pushed it open with the side of my body, and eased inside. I felt for the light switch and flicked it on.

"There's only one bedroom, but you can stay there."

"Thank you." She swallowed hard. "I didn't mean to inconvenience you. It should only take a day or two, then I'll leave."

"It's no problem." I settled her on my bed and opened my closet. I handed her a pair of pants, socks, and a t-shirt. "They're big but I suppose it's better than nothing." I tried for humor but it didn't work.

She took the clothing graciously and nodded. "Thank you."

"I'm going to get my medical supplies and remove that arrow." I didn't wait for her reply as I closed the door and fetched my first aid kit.

Grab your copy...
www.vinci-books.com/ladyhawk

About the Author

A Multi-genre author writing twisted endings...

N Gray is a USA Today Bestselling Author who lives in Cape Town, South Africa, with her daughter and adopted cat named Miss Beans.

During the day, she's an analyst and provider profiler for a medical insurance company. At night, she types on her curved keyboard, creating fictional characters some may love and others you want to kill yourself.

She writes in four genres: urban fantasy, thriller, horror, and paranormal romance.

She now writes under Natalie Michaels for her new thrillers and SD Syns for her new horrors.

Acknowledgments

Thank you to my readers, old and new, for taking a chance on my books.

You are the reason I write the stories I do. As long as you keep reading, I'll keep writing.

I'm truly humbled by your support and encouragement.

I write in as many genres as I love reading in. There are so many stories swarming inside my head that I could never just choose one.

Horror is my guilty pleasure. I love writing short stories filled with dark humour and the occult, with a twist ending.

Urban fantasy and paranormal romance are where I love to spend my time, and I have so many books planned that I don't have enough time *(but I'll get there)*.

And lastly, my thrillers. Who doesn't love sitting on the edge of their seat while reading about what goes on inside the antagonist's mind? Well, I love writing about them.